James Hadley Chase and The Murder Room

》》》 This title is part of The Murder Room, our series dedicated to making available out-of-print or hard-to-find titles by classic crime writers.

Crime fiction has always held up a mirror to society. The Victorians were fascinated by sensational murder and the emerging science of detection; now we are obsessed with the forensic detail of violent death. And no other genre has so captivated and enthralled readers.

Vast troves of classic crime writing have for a long time been unavailable to all but the most dedicated frequenters of second-hand bookshops. The advent of digital publishing means that we are now able to bring you the backlists of a huge range of titles by classic and contemporary crime writers, some of which have been out of print for decades.

From the genteel amateur private eyes of the Golden Age and the femmes fatales of pulp fiction, to the morally ambiguous hard-boiled detectives of mid twentieth-century America and their descendants who walk our twenty-first century streets, The Murder Room has it all. **》》》**

The Murder Room
Where Criminal Minds Me

themurderroom.com

T0352519

James Hadley Chase (1906–1985)

Born René Brabazon Raymond in London, the son of a British colonel in the Indian Army, James Hadley Chase was educated at King's School in Rochester, Kent, and left home at the age of 18. He initially worked in book sales until, inspired by the rise of gangster culture during the Depression and by reading James M. Cain's *The Postman Always Rings Twice*, he wrote his first novel, *No Orchids for Miss Blandish*. Despite the American setting of many of his novels, Chase (like Peter Cheyney, another hugely successful British noir writer) never lived there, writing with the aid of maps and a slang dictionary. He had phenomenal success with the novel, which continued unabated throughout his entire career, spanning 45 years and nearly 90 novels. His work was published in dozens of languages and over thirty titles were adapted for film. He served in the RAF during World War II, where he also edited the RAF Journal. In 1956 he moved to France with his wife and son; they later moved to Switzerland, where Chase lived until his death in 1985.

By James Hadley Chase
(published in The Murder Room)

You're Dead Without Money

James Hadley Chase

An Orion book

Copyright © Hervey Raymond 1972

The right of James Hadley Chase to be identified as the author of this
work has been asserted in accordance with the Copyright, Designs and
Patents Act 1988.

This edition published by
The Orion Publishing Group Ltd
Orion House
5 Upper St Martin's Lane
London WC2H 9EA

An Hachette UK company
A CIP catalogue record for this book is available from the British Library

ISBN 978 1 4719 0378 6

www.orionbooks.co.uk

1

With the temperature down to sub-zero and snow piling up on the sidewalks, to me New York had become a hole in the head. I longed for the sun. I hadn't been to Paradise City for two years and I now had the itch to relax in the comfort and luxury of the Spanish Bay Hotel – the best hotel on the Florida Coast.

I had sold a couple of shorties to the *New Yorker* and my last novel had been third on the Best-seller list for the past six months so I didn't have to worry about money. Looking out of my window at the grey sky, the snow and watching people moving around like ants far below me in a freezing wind gave me the incentive to reach for the telephone.

A telephone can be a miracle of convenience. You get an idea and the telephone will turn that idea into a reality – always providing you have money. I had money, so in a few minutes I was speaking to Jean Dulac who runs the Spanish Bay Hotel at Paradise City. In another few minutes, a room with a balcony that caught ten hours of sunshine per day and overlooking the sea was reserved for me.

Thirty-six hours later I arrived at Paradise City airport to be met by a gleaming white Cadillac that conveyed me to this fabulous hotel which catered only for fifty guests – each guest getting VIP treatment.

I spent my first week relaxing in the sun, chatting up the dollies and eating too much, then I remembered Al Barney.* Two years ago, I had met this fat, beer bloated beachcomber and he had given me an idea for a book. Barney described himself as a man with his ear to the ground. What he didn't know about the background, the crime, the sex-life and the muck behind the City wasn't worth knowing about.

I asked Dulac if Barney was still around.

'Of course.' He smiled. 'Paradise City without Al Barney would be like Paris without the Eiffel Tower. You will find him, as always, outside or inside the Neptune Tavern.'

So after an excellent dinner, I went down to the smelly waterfront with its crowd of camera festooned tourists, its fishermen and its fishing boats: one of the most picturesque scenes along the Florida coast.

I found Al Barney sitting on a bollard outside the shabby Neptune Tavern. He was still wearing the tattered dirty sweatshirt and the grease encrusted trousers he had been wearing when I first met him. Someone had patched the sweatshirt and had made a bad job of it – probably he had done it himself. An empty beer can in his enormous hand, he sat like a bloated piece of flotsam with the crowd of tourists moving around him.

To say Al Barney had seen better days would be to make one of the world's great understatements. Looking at him now, he just had to have had better days. I had been told by Dulac that at one time Barney ran a skin diving school and had been an expert skin diver. To see him as he sat on this bollard, this was hard to believe. Beer had mined him. Enormous, bloated, his face almost black by years of the

*See An Ear To The Ground.

2

Florida sun, his head balding, his small, blue eyes restlessly hunting for any opportunity for the fast buck, he sat there like a vulture in search of a sucker.

He saw me coming.

I knew by the way he stiffened, tucking in his great belly and tossing the beer can into the sea that he remembered me. He regarded me like a man lost in a desert would regard a long sought for oasis.

'Hi, Barney,' I said, coming to rest beside him. 'Remember me?'

He nodded and his little mouth that reminded me of the mouth of a red snapper went through the motions of a smile.

'Yeah ... sure I remember you. I have a good memory.' His eyes were now quizzing. 'It's Mr Campbell ... the writer.'

'Half way there. The writer part is right ... the name is Cameron,' I said.

'Yeah ... Cameron ... I remember. If there's one thing I'm good at it's people's faces. I gave you the dope about the Esmaldi diamonds ... right?'

'That's what you did.'

He scratched one of his hairy arms.

'Did you write a book about it?'

I wasn't that much of a sucker. I shook my head.

'Well, it was a good story.' He scratched some more, then he looked towards the door leading into the Neptune Tavern. 'I'm a guy with his ear to the ground. You want to hear something new?'

I said I was always interested in hearing anything new.

'You want to hear about the Larrimore stamps?' He stared at me, his eyes probing.

'Stamps ... what's new about stamps?' I asked.

3

'Yeah ... a good question.' He put his hand under his sweatshirt and scratched his belly. 'You know anything about stamps, mister?'

I admitted I knew nothing about stamps.

He nodded and withdrew his hand.

'I didn't either until I heard about the Larrimore stamps. I keep my ear to the ground. I have contacts. I have friends, newspapermen who talk. Even the cops talk and I listen.' He rubbed the back of his hand across his rubbery lips. 'You want to hear about it?'

I said stamps didn't interest me.

He nodded. 'That's right. They didn't interest me, but this is interesting. Let's go drink a beer.' He heaved himself to his feet. 'No one but me knows the complete story and I got it by keeping my ears open and my trap shut. Let's talk.' He moved through the crowd like a bulldozer through rubble. People either got out of his way or bounced off him as if hit by a truck. I followed him, knowing he was thinking about beer and when Al Barney thought of beer no one received his consideration except the guy who picked up the tab.

Sam, the Negro barman, was idly polishing a glass when we entered the Neptune Tavern and as soon as he saw me, his eyes lit up. He not only recognized me but he knew for some hours he would not only supply a lot of beer, but he would get paid for doing it, plus a tip.

'Evening, Mr Cameron, sir,' he said, beaming. 'Long time no see. Glad to have you around again, sir. What's it to be?'

'Two beers,' I said and because you did this sort of thing in Paradise City, I shook hands with him.

Barney had already settled his bulk on a bench by the window and was resting his elbows on the stained table. Sam produced two beers and brought them to the table. I

4

sat opposite Barney. I knew the procedure. Nothing was to be rushed. Before Barney would talk, his thirst had to be slaked. He drank the beer steadily and slowly, but not taking his lips from the glass until the glass was empty. Then he set down the glass, wiped his mouth with his forearm and released a long, soft sigh.

I didn't have to signal Sam. He was already at the table with the second beer.

'You know, mister, when a guy reaches my age,' Barney said, 'beer is a great consolation. There was a time when I went for women. Now, women mean nothing to me, but beer keeps me going.' He fingered his flat nose that was spread half over his face. 'If it hadn't been for a woman, I wouldn't have a sneezer like this. Her husband walked in on us and he was a puncher.' He shook his head as he reached for his glass. 'It was lucky for me he bust his fist on my snout ... otherwise I could have had a lot more trouble from him.'

I sipped my beer, then lit a cigarette. There was a pause while I thought of what Barney could have looked like in his heyday: an image impossible to conjure up.

'How's Mr Dulac?' Barney asked. 'I haven't seen him in weeks.'

'He's fine,' I said. 'He told me this City, without you, would be like Paris without the Eiffel Tower.'

Barney smirked.

'He's a gentleman ... I don't often say that ... most of the rich creeps living around here wouldn't know what the word "gentleman" means.' He emptied half his glass, then looked thoughtfully at me. 'Do you want to hear about Larrimore's Russian stamps, mister?'

'What's so interesting about them?'

'Anything worth a million dollars must be interesting,'
Barney said firmly. 'It beats me how bits of paper with
designs on them can get so valuable. It wasn't until I got all
the dope about these stamps that I realized what some
people do with them.' He leaned forward and poked a
finger as thick and as big as a banana in my direction. 'Did
you know some people behind the Iron Curtain use stamps
as their get away stake? Did you know some people put
their money in stamps to avoid income tax? Did you know
some people use stamps as foreign currency?'

I said I had heard such stories and what had this to do
with this man called Larrimore?

'It's a long story,' Barney said. 'I can give you all the
dope on the same terms we had last time ... that is if you
want the dope.'

I played hard to get. Stamps, I said, didn't interest me.

He finished his beer and rapped on the table. He didn't
have to alert Sam who was leaning on the bar watching
every sip. He came around, dumped another beer, then
went away, carrying the empty.

'I can understand that,' Barney said. 'You're not
interested in stamps because you don't know anything
about them. This is a story you could turn into a book. I'll
tell you something: if I could write, I wouldn't be giving it
to you. I'd be writing it myself, but as I can't write, I can do
a deal. How's about it?'

I said as I was on vacation with nothing better to do, I
would listen.

His little eyes became probing. 'The same terms as last
time?'

'Terms? What terms?'

6

He didn't hesitate. He might not have remembered my name, but he certainly remembered what he had screwed out of me for his last story.

'All the beer I want, some food, and a few bucks to take care of my time.'

'Okay,' and I parted with twenty dollars. He put the bills into his hip pocket as he signalled to Sam.

'You won't be disappointed, mister. Are you hungry?'

I said I wasn't hungry.

He shook his head, disapprovingly.

'When you get the chance to eat, mister, you should eat. You never know when the next meal is coming.'

I said I would bear this in mind.

There was a pause, then Sam brought over a three tier hamburger that oozed grease. He planted it before Barney who regarded it with a satisfied smirk. To me, it looked as appetizing as a drowned cat.

Barney began to munch while I waited. He took his time. After getting through the second tier of the hamburger and after finishing his beer, he sat back, rubbed his lips with his forearm and prepared to talk.

'A lot of people got involved in this stamp thing,' he said. 'To put you in the picture, I'll start with Joey Luck and his daughter, Cindy. Then I'll tell you about Don Elliot.' He paused to peer at me. 'You remember Don Elliot?'

'The movie star?'

Barney nodded. 'That's him. Did you ever see any of his movies?'

'Not my style. Didn't he take over Errol Flynn's mantle – a strictly cut and thrust performer?'

'You could say that, but he had his fans. He made six movies and they all made a pile of bread.'

'I haven't heard his name now for some years. What happened to him?'

'All in good time, mister, I'll get around to him later. I want you to get this story in its right perspective.' Barney looked anxiously at Sam who was pouring another beer. 'Step by step – one thing at the time. For you to understand this set up I've got to tell it my way.'

I said that was fine with me and would he get on with it?

'I'll start with Joey Luck and his daughter, Cindy, short for Lucinda, because they play a big part in the Larrimore stamp steal.' He looked slyly at me. 'I bet you never heard that this one million dollars' worth of stamps were stolen?'

I said if I had heard it would have been no skin off my nose.

Barney frowned. He wanted to create drama and he wasn't getting the right reaction so far from me.

'I'll get around to the steal in due time.' He paused to attack the third tier of his hamburger which had become a revolting looking mess of congealed grease. After he had munched a while, he squared himself on the bench, rested his enormous hands on the table and leaned forward. I could see he was at last ready to shoot in earnest. 'Joey Luck ... now the only thing lucky about Joey was his name,' he began. 'He was a dip.' He paused. 'You know what a dip is, mister?'

I said a dip was a man who put his hands in people's pockets and stole what he found there.

'That's exactly right. Joey was a small time dip. If he picked up a hundred dollars a week, which he seldom did, he thought he was Henry Ford. From way back, Joey always thought and acted small, but this made him smart because he acted so small the cops never got on to him. There're plenty of dips who act big and land up behind the

8

walls, but not Joey. He didn't even have a record. Now, I want you to understand, Mr Campbell, that Joey ...'

I thought I had better get this straightened out once and for all so I interrupted him to remind him my name was Cameron.

'That's right ... Cameron ... yeah.' He scratched the end of his nose, shifted on his seat and then went on, 'As I was saying, Joey wasn't a bad sort of guy. In fact you could say that he was a nice guy. I got along with him. When he had a bit of extra money, which wasn't often, he would buy a friend a beer. I would like you to get a picture of Joey: tall, thin with a lot of greying hair. He had one of those nondescript faces you see every day on any busy sidewalk: a face you don't remember, a face you don't look at twice. He always wore a shabby grey suit and a battered straw hat. He was around fifty years of age. He married young and his wife died giving birth to a baby girl who he called Lucinda. From what I hear Joey never got along with his wife so her loss didn't bother him. He was crazy about Cindy. He gave her a decent education and made no secret to her about what he was. Cindy adored him, and as soon as she left school, she became his partner. He taught her all his tricks, and by the time she was eighteen she was as good a dip as he was which is saying something. During the summer months they worked in New York, but when winter came, they moved down here. There was plenty to work on here, but they kept their operations small, living decently, but with no ambition to get rich.' He paused to stare at the beer in his glass, then went on, 'I'll give you a picture of Cindy. At the age of twenty, she was sensational. I've seen lots of girls of her age in my time, but none of them were a patch on Cindy. Like her old man, she was tall. She was blonde, with a traffic stopping figure and a pair of legs that cause car accidents.

Her looks bothered Joey. He knew sooner or later a man would turn up and he would lose her. This became a nightmare thing for Joey. He just couldn't imagine life without her. Up to the age of twenty, Cindy showed no interest in boyfriends. She could have had her pick, but she didn't play. Going around with Joey, dipping, keeping the home nice seemed to satisfy her. Joey prayed this would last, but he knew he was kidding himself.

'To put you more in the picture, I'll give you a brief idea of a routine day in their lives. They got up late and over coffee they discussed the menu of the day. They believed in eating well, but at the low expense of the various self-service stores in the district. Joey had dreamed up a smart idea of getting all the food and drink they required, not only for nothing but without risk. He had made a lightweight oval shaped basket with an open top which Cindy strapped to her tummy. Over this she wore a maternity dress. Leaning on her father's arm, her make-up pale, she looked the part of a brave little woman about to have her first baby. Not only did they jump all queues, but they lulled all suspicion while Cindy stowed away in the basket the best cuts of meat and the necessary accessories to a good meal while Joey's lean frame sheltered her activities from prying eyes. It was a nice little racket and provided them with good food for nothing. They then returned to their pad and while Cindy cooked lunch, Joey read aloud items from the newspaper which he considered of interest. After lunch they would separate. Cindy would work the stores while Joey worked the buses. They would meet again around five o'clock, with enough money to eat out in the evening and put a little by for the rainy day. Then they would watch TV until bedtime and the following day would be a repeat of the previous day. Not what you could call an exciting way of life, but it suited them.' Barney nodded to Sam who had just put down another beer. 'The time came for their move down here. They had rented a small bungalow on a five year lease on Seaview Boulevard – nothing very special but they liked it, being people, as I have said, without ambition. They arrived, settled in and began the same routine as when they lived in New York.' Barney paused to sip his beer. 'But this trip to Paradise City was to be different. This was when Joey's luck began to run out. The thing which he dreaded happened. Cindy fell in love.' Barney ran his finger around his plate, then conveyed the grease-laden finger to his mouth.

I asked him if he would like another hamburger.

'Not right now, thank you, but maybe a little later,' he said. 'Well, Cindy fell in love and this brings Vin Pinna on the scene. Although Pinna was only twenty-six years of age, he was a veteran in crime. He specialized in burglary and there were few locks, alarms or security guards he couldn't cope with. He made a decent living, ran a Jaguar car, travelled a lot and kept on the move so the police of the various states didn't catch up with him. The trouble with Vin was he couldn't hold on to money. As soon as he got paid by some fence he promptly spent the money on clothes, high living and dollies. In his way, he was a looker: tall, handsome, tough and vicious. He wore his hair long as they do these days and he spent a lot of money on this cock-eyed gear young guys of today like to wear. He had come to Paradise City for a look around. It's no secret that this City is stuffed with people who have more money than sense and the villas up on the hill are crammed to the ceiling with valuable loot.

'Before coming to Paradise City, Vin had been working Miami. While leaving a Miami hotel bedroom with some

11

old dowager's jewel box he had the bad luck to walk into the hotel dick. He knocked the dick cold. In the struggle he dropped the jewel box, but he got away. He knew the dick would give the cops a good description of him so he decided to move on and he moved here.

'Cindy spotted him as he was buying himself some neckties in one of the best stores in the City. She thought he was a real doll, but that didn't stop her trying for his billfold. There must have been something about Vin that spoilt her concentration because he felt her fingers slide into his hip pocket.

'He turned and smiled at her. They looked at each other and this chemistry thing called love clicked in her. She handed him back his billfold with a nice apology and accepted his offer of an ice drink. They talked for the rest of the afternoon until Cindy realized she should have been home an hour ago. This threw her into a panic. Not only had she been chatting up this handsome guy for hours but she had neglected her afternoon's work and had earned no money. This she explained to Vin who laughed and gave her twenty bucks, telling her he wanted to see her the following afternoon.

'Vin was pretty blasé about girls, but Cindy got to him. I'm not saying he fell in love with her as she had with him, but he liked her better than any other girl he had met and he wanted to see her again.

'Cindy agreed to meet him at the Lido where they could swim and talk. She had made no secret about what her father and she did for a living. Vin had been genuinely amused and he hinted he was in the crime racket himself although he didn't go into details. Cindy was impressed as he drove off in his Jaguar. Not only was he handsome, fun and sexy, she thought as she made her way home, but he was rich.

'Joey was quick to spot something had happened when Cindy came in. There was that far away look in her eyes that girls get when they are turning soppy over some man.' Barney paused to heave a great sigh. 'The number of times, when I was young, I've seen that look would surprise you. Like me, Joey knew the signs and a cold wind blew over him although he was smart enough not to ask questions.

'During the next six days, Cindy and Vin met every afternoon and by that time they were both crazy about each other.

'Then Cindy decided it was time to break the news to Joey. She dreaded telling him, but it had to be done. She couldn't go on deceiving him. She explained all this to Vin and asked him to meet her father. At first, Vin said no, but Cindy pleaded and because he wanted to please her, he shrugged and agreed.

' "Be nice to him, Vin," Cindy said. "He's been a wonderful father to me. Come around tomorrow at midday. That will give me time to break the news and get him in the right mood."

' "Okay ... okay," Vin said indifferently. "I'll come. I wouldn't do it for any other doll, but for you, I'll make the exception."

'Joey knew he was going to be told by the nervous way Cindy behaved when she came home. Joey had had six days in which to get used to the idea that Cindy was finally in love. He had told himself over and over again this was inevitable and he now knew if he wasn't to lose Cindy he would have to play his cards carefully. This could be calf love: something that wouldn't last, but he doubted it. He decided there was only one thing to do: he had to be understanding, pretend to be happy for Cindy and hope the guy came up to expectations and wouldn't let Cindy down.

13

The thought of spending the rest of his days on his own depressed him, but this he knew he would have to accept. If he could persuade Cindy not to rush into marriage, he would try, but he would try gently.

'After supper, instead of turning on the TV set, Joey said quietly, "What's on your mind, baby? Something you want to tell me?"

'So Cindy told him.

'Joey nodded.

' "It happens all the time and it had to happen to you. If you're happy, then that makes me happy, but are you sure?"

'Cindy went to him and put her arms around him.

' "I was scared of telling you. I thought you'd be angry."

' "What's there to be angry about? A girl like you should get married." Joey forced a smile. "Besides, I want to be a grandfather. I like kids. When's the wedding to be?"

'Cindy's eyes opened wide.

' "We're not planning to get married yet. We just want to be together, have fun ... we don't want kids for heaven's sake – anyway, not yet."

'Joey suppressed a sigh of relief.

' "But you do plan to get married, baby?"

' "We haven't discussed that," Cindy frowned. "We just want to have fun."

'Joey nodded.

' "Well, tell me about him."

'He listened to Cindy's eulogy, his heart despairing and his face alight with false interest.

' "He's a big operator," she concluded. "He hasn't told me just what his racket is, but it must be big. He's a terrific dresser and drives this big Jag and he's free with his money. You'll love him, dad. I'm sure you will."

14

'Joey said he hoped he would. Then after a pause, he asked if Vin had a record.

' "A record? What do you mean?" Cindy stiffened.

' "Well, you know ... do the cops know him ... has he ever been inside?"

' "I'm sure he hasn't! Of course not! Vin's much too smart to have a record."

' "That's fine." Joey hesitated, then went on, "We have to be careful, baby. So far we have kept clear of the cops. The bigger the operator the more dangerous he is."

' "I don't know what you mean!" Cindy had never spoken so sharply to her father before and Joey inwardly cringed.

' "I don't mean anything, baby. I just said we had to be careful."

' "We are careful. I can't see what Vin has to do with it. I tell you ... he's as smart as a whip."

'From his long experience in petty crime, Joey knew those who were smart as a whip were those who invariably got caught, but he didn't say so. He could only hope now that this affair wouldn't last long.

'When Cindy said Vin was coming to lunch the following day, Joey told her he was delighted.'

Barney leaned forward and looked over at Sam. He pointed to his enormous belly and wig-wagged with his eyebrows.

'If it's all the same to you, mister,' he said. 'I'll have another hamburger.'

* * *

The meeting between Joey and Vin went off better than either man expected. Joey certainly leaned over backwards to be pleasant, knowing Cindy was listening to every word he uttered and watching every change of his expressions. There was something about Vin that impressed Joey: his self confidence, the determined light in his steel grey eyes and the suggestion of ruthlessness told Joey this was no ordinary small time crook. He also realized that Vin seemed genuinely fond of Cindy and this pleased him: at least, his adored daughter wasn't going to be given the run-around.

Rather to his surprise, Vin found Joey easy to talk to, quick witted and in no way the heavy father.

The lunch which was elaborate was a success. After the meal, Vin took them in his Jag up in the hills, away from the crowded beach and went out of his way to make Joey feel he wasn't the odd man out.

Around 16.00, Joey who had enjoyed talking about his past life, telling Vin some of his varied experiences, said it was time for him to go to work.

'You take the day off, baby,' he said to Cindy. 'You and Vin have a little fun.'

They drove back to the City and dropped Joey off at the bus station. As they drove away, Cindy looked anxiously at Vin.

He grinned at her.

'He's a nice old guy,' he said. 'Small time – but I like him.' He put his hand on Cindy's. 'We three are going to get along fine together.'

That's the way it turned out. After a week, Joey suggested that Vin should move in with them at the bungalow. After some thought, Joey had decided he could see more of Cindy if Vin moved in and besides, he found he liked having Vin around to talk to. He didn't realize until now how he had been missing male conversation.

After hesitating, Vin agreed. He was getting a little worried about his financial position. He was staying at a modest hotel, but the rates of even a modest hotel in Paradise City came high. Before very long, he told himself he would have to do a job. Up to now, he had been content to enjoy Cindy's company. He refused to admit to himself that the encounter with the hotel dick had shaken his nerve. He decided he would give hotels a wide berth. He must tackle one of these villas he had heard so much about. So when Joey suggested he take one of the spare bedrooms and contribute twenty dollars a week to help out, Vin, after checking his billfold and finding he was down to his last five hundred dollars, agreed.

All the same, although pressure was now relaxed on his billfold, Vin told himself he must get down to work. He was a stranger in Paradise City and had no connections which made things tricky. He knew Joey and Cindy had been coming to the City for the past three years and he decided to have a word with Joey to find out if Joey could steer him to a steal.

So one morning while Cindy was preparing the lunch and the two men sat under the shade of a tree in the little garden, Vin casually asked if Joey knew of a reliable fence in the City.

'Fence? There are several.' Joey shook his head. 'I wouldn't say they are reliable. The best fence is Claude Kendrick. He runs a big antique shop in the swank district of the City, but he is strictly big time. He supplies antiques and modern art to most of the big shots living around here and makes a fortune, but he also deals in hot goods. It depends, of course, what he's offered. Give him something top class and he'll take it, but not small stuff. Abe Levi who runs a tourist junk shop takes the small stuff, but he pays badly. All the same, I should think Abe would be the man for you.' Joey looked thoughtfully at Vin. 'Are you thinking of pulling a job?'

17

'My dough's running out,' Vin said, frowning. 'Yes, I've got to do a job.'

This was a shock to Joey although he was careful not to show it. He had been under the impression from what Cindy had told him that Vin was larded with the stuff and now to hear Vin was running short, more than depressed him.

'Look, Vin,' he said. 'Don't do anything rash. I ...'

Vin's sudden scowl stopped him short. For the first time, Joey saw the meaner side of Vin's nature and this was also a shock.

'Rash? I don't get you,' Vin growled. 'When I pull a job, I do it right.'

'I'm sure you do,' Joey said hastily, 'but you're in Paradise City now, Vin. This City's special. It's like a closed shop if you know what I mean.'

Vin stared at him.

'Like a ... what?'

'The boys here have everything organized,' Joey explained, his tone apologetic. 'Outsiders aren't encouraged.'

Vin stiffened and his eyes hardened.

'Is that right? Am I an outsider?'

Joey fidgeted with his beautifully shaped hands.

'I guess you are, Vin. The boys won't take kindly to you if you start operating here.'

'So what will they do if I do operate?'

Joey ran his fingers through his thick, grey hair.

'From what I hear they will tip the cops, and Vin, make no mistake about this, the cops here are dynamite. It's their job to protect the rich living here and believe me, they do a job.'

Vin lit another cigarette. He thought for a long moment, then, his voice more subdued, he asked, 'So how do I get an in, Joey?'

Joey looked unhappy.

'It's tricky, but talk to Abe. Tell him you're in the business and ask him politely what he can do for you. It's the only way, Vin. If Abe turns you down, that's it. You must not operate in this City. If you do, without Abe's say-so, you're certain to get picked up by the cops.'

'I never had this trouble in Miami,' Vin said angrily. 'What the hell's with it with this goddamn City?'

'Take an older man's tip then,' Joey said. 'Live here and work Miami. It's not all that far away. You could spend a couple of days there, do a job and come back here.'

Vin shook his head.

'Miami's too hot for me now,' he said sullenly. 'I've got to work this City if I'm going to work at all.'

Joey shifted uneasily in his chair.

'You're not in trouble?'

'Trouble? No, but the cops in Miami have a description of me. I can't go back there.' Vin stared up at the blue sky. 'I'll tell you something. I'm getting sick of this way of life, Joey. As soon as I get any money I either lose it or spend it. I want to do a once-and-for-all job that will set me up for three or four years ... I want to marry Cindy. I want to buy a bungalow somewhere on this coast and for us three to settle there. You and me could go fishing and we could talk. Cindy and I could have fun and you could stick around because I like you, Joey. I wouldn't want you to leave us. We've talked about it. When Cindy and I want to be alone I'd give you the high sign and because you're smart you'd leave us alone. That way we could all live together and have fun.'

Joey couldn't believe his ears. This was what he had been praying and hoping for. Tears rushed into his eyes and he had to get out his handkerchief and pretend he was stifling a sneeze.

19

'But, first, I've got to pull a big one,' Vin went on, not noticing Joey's emotion. 'It's got to be big. Fifty thousand dollars would do it. Now how the hell am I going to find a job worth all that bread?'

Fifty thousand dollars!

Joey sat up in alarm.

'Now look, Vin, that's kid's talk. Fifty grand! They could put you away for fifteen years. Now get that right out of your mind! You don't think I want a son-in-law locked away for fifteen years, do you?'

Vin stared at him, his eyes cloudy and far away. He didn't have to put into words the thought that was going through his mind. Joey knew Vin was regarding him with friendly contempt and Vin knew he was looking at a man who lived and thought small and would always live and think small.

Cindy came to the open door that led to the living-room.

'Come and get it,' she called.

As the two men got to their feet, Vin asked, 'Where do I find Abe Levi?'

*　　*　　*

Abe Levi's junk shop was located on the waterfront near where the sponge trawlers and the lobster boats anchored. The shop was one of the City's tourists' attractions. It contained anything from a stuffed snake to a tortoiseshell comb, from glass 'diamonds' to handicrafts made by the local Indians, from a canoe to the original muzzle loader that killed some General during the Indian wars. You name it, Levi had it.

Stuffed with objects, the vast, dimly lit shop was served by four attractive Seminole girls, wearing their native costumes. Levi kept behind the scenes in his small, pokey office. Although Levi made a large and steady income from the junk he sold, he made an even larger and even more steady income from handling loot the local thieves offered him and at a much bigger profit.

Abe Levi was tall and thin with a balding head, a hooked nose and eyes as impersonal as bottle stoppers.

He regarded Vin as Vin sat by Abe's old fashioned roll top desk and what Abe saw he didn't like. He didn't like handsome men. He dealt with the small fry of the City's thieves who were invariably shabby and far from handsome. This tall, bronzed man in his immaculate suit and outrageous tie and his arrogance made Abe instinctively hostile.

Vin had explained who he was and that he was looking for a job to pull. Abe listened, stroking his hooked nose with thin boney fingers, shooting quick glances at Vin and then looking away.

'If I find something,' Vin concluded, 'are you in the market to buy?'

Abe didn't hesitate.

'No.'

The flat note and the hostile expression sent a wave of hot anger up Vin's spine.

'What do you mean?' he snarled. 'You're in the goddamn business, aren't you?'

Abe fixed Vin with his bottle stopper eyes.

'I'm in the business but not to outsiders. There's nothing here for you in this City. Try Miami. They take outsiders. We don't.'

'Is that right?' Vin leaned forward, his big hands into fists. 'If you don't want my business, there are plenty who will.'

Abe continued to stroke his nose.

'Young man, don't do it,' he said. 'This City is a closed shop. We have enough working here without outsiders. Go to Miami, but don't try to operate here.'

'Thanks for nothing. So I operate here,' Vin said, red showing through his bronze. 'Who's going to stop me?'

'The cops,' Abe said. 'The cops here know there must be a certain amount of crime in this City. They accept this, but they don't accept a new face. Someone will tip them that a new face has arrived and the owner of the new face has ideas. In a few days that new face is either run out of the City or else lands up behind bars. Take my tip: there's nothing here for you. Go to Miami. That's a fine city for a young man like you – but don't try anything here.'

Vin stared for a long moment at this tall, thin Jew and it dawned on him that this old man was being helpful in his odd way. He lifted his shoulders and stood up.

'Well, thanks,' he said. 'I'll think about it,' and turning, he made his way through the shop, ignoring the Indian girls who were ogling him hopefully and into the hot sunlight of the waterfront.

For the first time in his life, he felt a lack of confidence and a nagging fear that soon his money would run out. He didn't want to leave Paradise City. He wanted to be with Cindy. But what was he to do? He knew a warning when he was given a warning and Abe Levi had shown him the red light.

With lagging steps, he walked to where he had parked the Jaguar.

2

A middle aged, fat, blonde woman, followed by a man who could have been her husband came into the bar. They climbed up on stools and ordered whisky on the rocks. The man, weedy, balding, wearing a bush jacket and crumpled khaki slacks divested himself of two expensive looking cameras which were festooned around his neck. He stared around and his eyes finally came to rest on Barney who was putting away the third tier of his second hamburger.

The weedy man nudged the fat blonde who swivelled her head and eyed Barney, her pale blue eyes popping. This woman had managed to wedge her enormous hips into a pair of flame coloured shorts. I felt that any extra movement from her would make the shorts give at the seams. Over her vast frontage, she had on a light weight sweater with a pattern of orange rings against a white background.

'One of the local characters, Tim,' she said in a loud whisper. 'I love this City. You can't move a yard without finding something exciting to look at.'

Barney looked a little smug. 'You know, Mr Campbell, people notice me,' he said. 'Mr Dulac is right. I am a tourist attraction.' He pointed his big finger at my chest. 'I'll bet you a nickel before those two leave, the punk will want to take my photograph.'

I said it was a bet, but how about getting on with this story of his?

Barney nodded.

'Yeah ... well, you know about Joey, Cindy and Vin. We'll leave them for the moment with the outlook for Vin bleak. He could, of course, have moved on to Jacksonville and tried his luck there, but he now had this rooted idea that he had to pull off the big one so he could settle with Cindy and Joey for at least a couple of years before looking for another job, and he knew Paradise City was about the only city apart from Miami where you could find loot worth fifty thousand bucks in one quick, safe steal.'

Seeing the fat woman was still gaping at him, Barney wigwagged with his bushy eyebrows and gave her a leering grin. The woman looked hastily away and leaning close to her husband, she began to whisper.

'She's a little shy,' Barney said. 'You wait. They'll be over here wanting my photo.' As I said nothing, he went on, 'Now I'll tell you about Don Elliot. You've seen plenty of pictures of him: a tall, well built guy, handsome, dark and with that sexy look most women can't resist.

'When Errol Flynn kicked off, there was an opening for a movie actor to take his place. Pacific Pictures had Elliot under contract and they realized, with careful grooming, they could move him into Flynn's market. They groomed him and he delivered. His first three movies went well and did big box office. He was a mixture of Flynn and Fairbanks senior. As you said, no actor, but a good cut and thrust merchant. His agent, Sol Lewishon, was smart enough to get Elliot on a percentage deal after the third movie and Elliot really moved into the dough. Like most movie stars, he was a heavy spender.' Barney paused to eat the last of the hamburger. 'It's an odd thing with these movie people. They have this inferiority complex. You know what I mean?' He stared at me with his small, calculating eyes. 'They think if they don't live it up the rest of the world will think they're cheapies. They have to have big cars, flash women, big houses, swimming pools. They have to throw their money around. Elliot was like that. He came to Paradise City and built a villa up on the hill and this villa, Mr Campbell, sure as death, had everything. I heard it cost around half a million bucks. Maybe that's an exaggeration, maybe not. It wasn't all that big, but it had everything. One of my newspaper friends wrote an article about the villa and he showed me some of the photos.' Barney drew in a long slow breath. 'It had every gimmick you can imagine. Four bedrooms, four bathrooms and a living-room that could hold two hundred people without them breathing down each other's necks, a dining hall, swimming pool, a play room, sauna baths, barbecue – you name it, Elliot had it. He even had his own movie theatre.

'He had three cars: a Rolls, an Alfa and a Porsche racer. He was a sociable guy and he was liked. The rich creeps living here entertained him and were entertained by him. His movies were great box office. Things looked set for him, but as so often happens, his luck ran out.'

At this moment the fat woman and her weedy husband finished their drinks and got off their stools. Barney looked at me and winked, then sat back, preening himself, stroking out the wrinkles in his sweatshirt. The fat woman and her husband went out of the bar without looking at him and they disappeared into the crowd moving along the waterfront. There was a long pause, then I said gently that he owed me a nickel.

Barney shook his head in disbelief.

'That's never happened before. If I told you the number of times I've been photographed by these tourist jerks you wouldn't believe it.'

'A nickel,' I said.

He dismissed this with a wave of his hand.

'Let's get back to Don Elliot,' he said firmly and rapped his empty glass on the table. He waited until Sam had brought him a refill, then went on, 'As I was saying, Elliot's luck ran out. He had completed six movies and Pacific Pictures were drafting a new contract that would give him 20% of the producer's profits, and that, from what I have been told, would have netted him a million bucks, plus all expenses and so on and so on. The contract was finally ready to sign, and Lewishon, his agent, called him from Hollywood and asked him to come on up and sign it. At this time, Elliot had found another doll he imagined he was in love with. I saw her: a good looking chick if you like them skinny: blonde, of course, with flashing green eyes and tits that should have been muzzled. The two of them left here in the racing Porsche for Hollywood. Half way to Hollywood, the girl wanted to drive. As Elliot was nuts about her, he let her. She had no more idea of handling a racing car than I have. At around a hundred and five miles an hour, she hit a truck. His safety belt saved him, but she took the steering wheel messily in her chest. When Elliot came to in a private, top class clinic, he found Sol Lewishon and the President of Pacific Pictures at his bedside.' Barney drank a little beer and persuaded his fat face to look sad. 'Maybe you read about it in the newspapers?' he asked.

I said I must have missed it. I didn't have much time to read newspapers and news from Hollywood seldom interested me.

Barney nodded.

'The chick was killed of course and they had a lot of trouble digging Elliot out of what was left of his car. To get him out, they had to cut off his left foot that had got caught in the wreckage.

'The President of Pacific Pictures, a guy called Meyer, told him not to worry, to get well and then come and see him. Then he left. He had only come because he wanted to be sure Elliot had really lost his foot. He couldn't believe it when the news had been relayed to him. One moment he had a big money spinner who jumped, ran, rode, swam, climbed, fought and did all the things Flynn had done and now he had a hunk of good looking flesh minus a foot.'

Barney sat back and regarded me.

'You get the photo, mister? A guy with a potential earning power of a million bucks suddenly without a foot. Quite a thing, huh?'

I agreed.

'Elliot was under sedation and had no idea he had lost his foot. Lewishon knew the goose that had been laying golden eggs for him was now washed up. He would have to hunt up another handsome hunk of flesh from somewhere and persuade Meyer to start grooming all over again and he knew he couldn't afford to waste time on Elliot. He broke the news to Elliot that he had lost a foot, said they must get together when Elliot left the clinic, said he would talk to Meyer and scrammed.

'A month later, Elliot was back in Paradise City. He came back a changed man: hard, sour and bitter. He didn't see any of his so called friends. He kept to himself. A couple of months later he was fixed up with a tin foot. He had a lot of guts and he really persevered with the tin foot. He got it so he could walk normally without a shade of a limp, but running, jumping, fighting and so on were now strictly for the birds. Also the tin foot gave him a complex. Before losing his foot he spent a lot of time with the dollies in his swimming pool, but you don't go swimming with a tin foot.

'Elliot used to lay some girl three or four times a week, but it is sort of embarrassing to get into bed with a doll when what should have been a foot is a red looking stump. But that was only a small piece of his troubles. As soon as he was satisfied he could walk normally, he took a plane to Hollywood and called on Lewishon. When he walked into his agent's office, Lewishon gaped at him. He had written Elliot off but seeing this big, sun bronzed handsome guy come in the way he used to come in revived Lewishon's hopes for more golden eggs.

'He immediately contacted Meyer, but Meyer knew Elliot was a non-starter. He knew Elliot had no acting talent. To him, a cut and thrust merchant with a tin foot was as saleable as a contraceptive to a eunuch. He said he was sorry, but no dice. To give him his due, Lewishon tried, but when Meyer said "no", he meant no.

'When Lewishon broke the news, Elliot stared at him, white faced. "So what the hell am I going to live on?" he demanded.

'Lewishon was puzzled that Elliot was taking this so badly.

' "What are you worrying about?" he asked impatiently. "You have royalties coming in on three movies. You can count on at least $30,000 a year for the next five years and a little less for another five years. You won't starve and who knows what'll happen after ten years – we could all be dead."

'Elliot's hands turned into fists.

' "I owe money everywhere," he said. "Thirty thousand is chick feed. I was relying on this new contract to get me out of my hole."

'Lewishon shrugged.

28

' "Sell the villa. You could raise half a million on that."

' "It's not mine, goddamn it! It's mortgaged to the roof!"

' "Okay, Don, let's get down to it. How much do you owe?"

'Elliot lifted his hands in despair.

' "I don't know, but it's plenty ... something like two hundred thousand ... probably more."

'Lewishon thought for a moment. He was a sharpie and he saw a chance of making a good investment. Elliot's six movies could bring in an income of around $30,000 for the next five years and after five years they could still bring in something. He said he might find someone (meaning himself) to buy the rights and pay Elliot $100,000 cash down.

'Elliot tried to get him to make it $150,000 and Lewishon said he would see what he could do. Elliot went back to Paradise City and waited.

'Finally, Lewishon persuaded him to accept the $100,000 and with his back to the wall, Elliot agreed. He got the cash, but from that moment he was out on a limb.

'The money went to settling some of his debts. There was something fatal about Elliot. He just couldn't stop spending. He should have cleared out of the villa and taken a small apartment. He should have got rid of his staff who he paid well and who ate their heads off. He shouldn't have ordered the new Rolls that cost around $30,000, promising to pay later.

'He knew he was heading for a god-awful crash, but there was nothing he seemed able to do to avoid it.

'At the back of his mind there was the thought of suicide. When the crash finally came, he told himself, he would empty a bottle of sleeping tablets down his throat and that would be that.

'If this was to be his end, he decided, then he would make hay while the sun shone. He began to entertain again. His

29

parties weren't the success they used to be because he wasn't the same man he used to be. His hard, cynical, jeering attitude bothered people. Nobody had an idea that he was without money. By now, everyone knew about his tin foot and that he was washed up in movies, but they believed he had stashed away enough when he was in the money to be still a very rich man.

'Then one day he got a call from his bank manager, asking him to drop in and have a talk. Elliot knew what this meant. He dropped in and had a talk. His account was in the red for twenty thousand dollars and the bank manager who often played golf with him said regretfully he couldn't give him any more credit. "Head Office is pressing me to get this overdraft reduced," he said. "What can you do about it, Don?"

' "Leave it to me," Elliot said. "I'll fix it," knowing he hadn't a hope in hell of fixing anything. "What's with your people, Jack? Twenty thousand is peanuts."

'The bank manager agreed but said his people were pressing him. "So let's reduce it by half, Don."

'Elliot said he would fix it and left.

'The Rolls coupe had been delivered the previous week: it was the only car of its kind in the City. Elliot had been offered it ahead of anyone else and he just couldn't resist taking it, knowing the car agent wouldn't press him too hard for payment. He found this magnificent car did a great deal to bolster up his sagging credit. He had only to drive up in the car to one of the stores or to his tailor for credit to be immediately granted.

'Then one day, his Japanese major-domo informed him his stock of whisky and gin was running low and reminded him that he was throwing a big cocktail party the following evening. Elliot got a shock when Fred Bailey who ran the liquor store asked him to settle his last account.

' "This has been running now for six months, Mr Elliot," Bailey explained apologetically. "It's six thousand dollars. Could I ask you ...?"

'Elliot gaped at him. He had no idea the parasites who he entertained had soaked up six thousand dollars' worth of drink over a period of six months.

' "I'll send you a cheque," he said airily. "Right now, Fred, I want four cases of Scotch and five of gin ... the usual. Get them over to my place by this afternoon, will you?"

'Bailey hesitated. Then looking out of the window at the Rolls, he reluctantly nodded. No one owning a car like that, he reasoned to himself, could be short of money.

' "Okay, Mr Elliot, but let me have that cheque. My people are pressing me."

'Elliot now realized time was running out for him. Back at the villa, he got out all the bills waiting payment and spent a bleak afternoon totalling them up. He found, give or take, he owed around $70,000 and this didn't include the Rolls.

'He sat back, worried, looking around the luxuriously furnished living-room. During his money-making days, he had bought modern paintings, expensive pieces of sculpture and among other things a collection of jade that had set him back in the region of $25,000. He had bought all this stuff from Claude Kendrick who I have already mentioned.' Barney paused to finish his beer, then squinted at me. 'You remember I mentioned Claude Kendrick?'

I said I remembered and that Joey Luck had said Kendrick was one of the top fences in the City.

Barney nodded approvingly.

'That's correct. I'm glad you're keeping close to me, Mr Campbell. You know something? There's nothing more discouraging to a guy with his ear to the ground than to talk to a deaf audience.'

That, I said, I could understand.

There was a pause while Sam brought another beer, then Barney began talking again.

'This is the moment to bring Claude Kendrick on the scene because he played a role in the Larrimore stamp steal.' Barney hitched himself forward. 'Let me give you a picture of Kendrick. He was a tall massively built queer of around sixty years of age and he wore an ill fitting orange wig and pale pink lipstick. He was as bald as an egg and wore this wig just for the hell of it. When he met one of his lady clients he would raise the wig like you would raise your hat – strictly a character, you understand, Mr Cambell? He was fat.' Barney slapped his enormous belly. 'Not the way I'm fat, you understand. My fat is good hard fat, but his was soft fat and that's no good to anyone. He had a long thick nose and little eyes and what with all this fat covering his face and this long snout he looked like a dolphin but without a dolphin's nice expression. Although he looked comic and acted comic, he was a top expert in antiques, jewellery and modern art. His gallery was crammed with outstanding *objets d'art* and collectors came from all over the world after a bargain.' Barney grinned. 'They got what they wanted, but never a bargain.

'Apart from this flourishing business, Kendrick was also a fence. He became a fence by force of circumstances you might say. Important clients came to him wanting some special art treasure that wasn't for sale. Their offer was so big, Kendrick couldn't resist. He found a couple of smooth operators who stole what was wanted and the collectors paid and kept whatever it was in their private museums for their eyes only. Some of the steals Kendrick organized would make your hair stand on end. He once organized the steal of a priceless Ming vase from the British Museum and that nearly got him into real trouble, but that's another story and I won't go into that now. I just want you to get the photo of how Kendrick operated.

'Apart from being a successful fence, he supplied most of the rich creeps living here with top class works of art. He had a way with him that inspired confidence. People sniggered about his orange wig and his make-up, but they came to him and were glad to have his advice. He had a team of beautiful boys who were experts in decor and he was always fixing and refixing people's homes.

'When Elliot built his villa, he had gone to Kendrick who had arranged the decor and had unloaded a mass of art – if you can call it that – on him as well as this jade collection, plus a lot of other stuff at very fancy prices.

'Elliot decided he could well do without the jade and come to that, all the freakish paintings that covered the walls of his living-room. He was now in desperate need for ready cash – not to pay his bills: these would have to wait – but to pay his staff and keep himself, and this seemed to him to be the way of getting it.

'After some hesitation, because he knew once you offered something for sale the word could get around you were in financial trouble, he drove down to Kendrick's gallery.'

*   *   *

Louis de Marney, Kendrick's head salesman, came forward as Elliot entered the gallery.

Louis was thin and willowy and could be any age from twenty-five to forty. His long thick hair was the colour of sable and his lean face, narrow eyes and almost lipless mouth made him look like a suspicious rat.

'Ah, Mr Elliot ... so good to see you again,' he gushed.

'Are you better now? Splendid ... splendid. I was utterly shattered when I heard of the accident. Did you get my letter? I wrote ... who didn't? But you look so well! How wonderful!'

'Claude around?' Elliot asked abruptly. He hated being gushed over and specially by a queer.

'Of course ... a little occupied. You know how it is? Dear Claude works himself to death. Is there something I can do, something I can show you, Mr Elliot?' The small eyes were probing, the lipless mouth revealed white teeth in a smile that didn't reach the eyes.

'I want Claude,' Elliot said. 'Hurry it up, Louis. I'm busy too.'

'Of course ... a tiny moment.'

Elliot watched him weave his way gracefully down the long aisle that led to Kendrick's reception room. Kendrick refused to call this room in which he did all his big deals an office: a vast room with a picture window looking out to the sea, sumptuously furnished with some of the most impressive and expensive antiques that Claude possessed with paintings worth a fortune hanging on the silk covered walls.

While he waited, Elliot moved uneasily around the vast gallery examining the various *objets d'art* set out temptingly in glass cases. During the three minutes he waited he spotted several things he felt the urge to buy, but he knew Kendrick never gave credit no matter how important the client.

Louis minced towards him.

'Please come ... Claude is so happy! You know, Mr Elliot, you have been neglecting us. It must be four months since you have visited us.'

'Yeah.' Elliot followed Louis' slim back. He entered Kendrick's reception room.

Claude Kendrick was standing by the window, staring down at the sea. He turned as Elliot came in and his fat face creased into a smile.

'What a freak!' Elliot thought. 'That god-awful wig! He's fatter than ever!'

'My very dear Don,' Kendrick said and enfolded Elliot's hand in both his. Elliot felt as if his hand had been thrust into a bowl of warm, slightly moist dough. 'How very good to see you again. You're naughty to have neglected me. How is the poor foot ... the poor darling?'

'I wouldn't know,' Elliot said. 'They dropped it in the furnace, I believe.' Moving away from Kendrick's overpowering massiveness, he sank on to a Louis XVI settee. 'How are things with you?'

'Fair ... let us say we don't grumble. We have much to be thankful for. And you, dear Don, how are things with you?' Kendrick paused, putting his head on one side and a sly look came into his little eyes. 'I heard about that dreadful Meyer – what a horrible man! I heard he won't renew your contract. That man! I wouldn't sell him one single thing in my beautiful gallery. He came to me once. He actually tried to bargain with me! There are people I can deal with and people I just can't. There are people who fill me with revulsion. Meyer is that sort of people. You understand ... of course you do! Is it true he won't renew your contract?'

'He would be crazy if he did,' Elliot said. 'Meyer's all right. He's in business to make money like you and me. I've got a tin foot, Claude, and that puts paid to my racket. I don't blame Meyer. I'd have done the same thing if I had been in his place.'

'There's no pity in this horrid world.' Kendrick grimaced. 'But what am I thinking of? A little champagne ... a whisky? Do have something?'

'No, thanks.'

There was a pause as Kendrick lowered his bulk into a special chair he had designed for himself: a wing backed chair, cleverly designed as an antique but reinforced with steel and covered with what looked like a Gobelin but was in fact a brilliant fake.

'Louis tells me you are busy so I won't keep you,' Elliot went on. 'You remember that jade collection you sold me?'

'The jade? Of course.' Kendrick's eyes turned watchful. 'A beautiful set. Do you want it cleaned, dear Don? Jade needs cleaning once in a while. It is so easy to neglect one's treasures.'

'I don't want it cleaned ... I want to sell it.'

Kendrick took off his wig, polished his bald head with a silk handkerchief, then replaced the wig a little crookedly.

'You look a hell of a sight in that goddamn wig,' Elliot said with a burst of irritation.

'It has a psychological effect on me,' Kendrick said. 'When I lost all my hair I was in despair. You have no idea, cheri, how I suffered. I have always despised stupid men wearing wigs to make them look younger. So I bought this abortion and I have fun with it and yet I don't go around bald. It is good for me and it amuses my friends and it gets talked about.'

Elliot shrugged. 'What about it? Are you in the market to buy jade?'

'Cheri! I can't believe you want to get rid of that lovely set! Perhaps you don't realize ... people talk about it. They envy you! It's been mentioned three times during the years in the *World of Art* ...'

'I want to sell it.' Elliot's face was wooden. 'What's it worth, Claude?'

A glazed look appeared in Kendrick's eyes: it was a look that came when he moved from seller to buyer.

'Worth?' He lifted his massive shoulders. 'It depends on who wants it. You appreciate it – I appreciate it. It is a rare and beautiful collection but it is, after all a specialized item. You don't find people interested in big jade collections every day in the week.' He paused to stare inquisitively at Elliot. 'Are you planning to trade it in for something else, Donny boy? Have you seen something in my beautiful gallery that has caught your fancy? That Spode collection for instance or ...'

'I want to sell it for cash,' Elliot said, 'and for God's sake, don't call me Donny boy.'

'So sorry. Cash?' Kendrick made a grimace making him look like a dolphin which had bitten into a hook. 'Well now, there's a problem. If you were thinking of trading it in for something else I would be able to make you a cosy offer, but for cash ...'

'How much?'

'I would have to see it again of course. People are so careless ... it could have got chipped, but if it is in mint condition – as I sold it to you – I think I could offer ... say, six thousand. Yes, I might go to six as you are a good friend of mine.'

Blood rushed into Elliot's face.

'What the hell are you talking about? You stuck me for twenty-five thousand six hundred!'

Kendrick lifted his fat hands and dropped them in a gesture of despair on his fat knees.

'But that was four years ago, dear Don. Prices have slumped, especially with jade. People aren't collecting jade any more. Good china: Spode ... Wedgwood ... there's interesting money there but not for the moment in jade. It'll come back, of course. In another two or three years I could offer you something that would give you a profit.' He appeared to hesitate, then went on, 'But, if you really want quick cash and because you are my friend, I'll take a risk. I will give you ten. That's the absolute top and I could live to regret it.'

Elliot shook his head. 'No. I'll try Miami. There are a couple of dealers there who could offer more. Okay, Claude ... forget it.'

'You're not thinking of Morris Hervey and Winston Ackland, are you, cheri?' Kendrick asked, his smile pityingly sad. 'You mustn't deal with them. Dreadful people and besides, they are up to their horrid eyes in jade. I did a deal with them three months ago before the bottom of the jade market dropped out. They would give you four.'

Elliot experienced a feeling of defeat. He had to have cash. Maybe ten thousand was better than nothing. The jade collection meant nothing to him now. In fact, it bored him.

'There's this other junk you sold me, Claude,' he said. 'I don't want to keep any of it. Right now, I want cash. How about taking the lot back?'

Kendrick got up and walked to the cocktail cabinet, a magnificent piece of furniture of mother of pearl and tortoiseshell inlay. He poured two stiff whiskies, added ice from the built-in refrigerator and put one of the glasses by Elliot's side. Then he sat down and regarded Elliot with what appeared to be genuine sympathy.

'Why not confide in me, dear Don? Things are tough? You owe money? You've been living too well? The wolf at the door?'

Elliot reacted to this as if he had been flicked with a whip.

'That's none of your goddamn business and I don't want your goddamn drink! I'm here to talk business ... let's talk business!'

'I'm your friend,' Kendrick said gently. 'Please remember that. Any confidence given to me goes no further. I could help you, cheri, but naturally I think I am entitled to know how you are situated.'

His quiet tone and his steady stare made Elliot realize that right now he was friendless. If this gross pansy with his ridiculous wig meant what he was saying, he could be crazy to ignore his offer to help.

After a moment's hesitation, he said, 'Okay, Claude, I'll tell you. The blunt fact is I'm broke and in debt. That damned Rolls isn't paid for. All I have to call my own is the stuff you sold me.'

Kendrick sipped his whisky.

'No prospects?'

'None. I'm washed up as a movie star. I've no acting talent. No – no prospects.'

'We mustn't look on the darkest side,' Kendrick said as he stroked his big nose. 'I won't waste time saying I'm sorry although I am. You did have prospects but you were unlucky. We all could be unlucky. At least, unlike so many unlucky people, you have up to now had a merry life. What you want is immediate help. Suppose I send Louis up to your place and get him to make an inventory of the things you have? It is some time since you bought from me and I forget just what you have.'

Elliot nodded. 'Okay, but I don't want Louis shooting his mouth around the City. It needs only a rumour that I'm in trouble for all my creditors to move in. I've got to have a lump of money by the end of the month ... three weeks.'

'What do you mean by a lump of money?'

'To get me straight, I need at least a hundred and fifty thousand dollars. If I don't get that, I'll go bust and then no one gets anything.'

Kendrick pursed his fat lips.

'That's quite a sum, but don't despair. Let's see what we can do. Louis will be with you tomorrow at ten. When he has made an inventory, we will have another talk.'

'There's that Chagall you unloaded on me. That would be worth a hell of a lot.'

Kendrick looked sad. 'Not a good one if I remember rightly. At that time people were crazy about any Chagall, but of course it has its value. You can rely on me. I will do my very best to be helpful.'

Elliot got to his feet. He hadn't much hope. He felt instinctively this could turn out to be a deal that would give him little and this fat queer much.

'Okay, Claude, then I'll leave it to you.'

'Yes.' Kendrick rubbed his smooth shaven jaw, then said casually, 'You know Paul Larrimore I believe?'

Surprised, Elliot stared at him.

'I know him ... what of it?'

'A difficult man to get to know,' Kendrick said, his fat face sad. 'Rather a recluse, wouldn't you say?'

'He keeps to himself if that's what you mean. I wouldn't call him a recluse. Why bring him up?'

'You and he, I understand, are friends.'

'I guess so. What's all this about?'

'I'm anxious to get into contact with him, but he refuses to see me. I find this a little churlish and I was wondering if you could break the ice for me.'

'Larrimore is tricky.' Elliot shook his head. 'He doesn't welcome people. What do you want with him?'

'Stamps.' Kendrick smiled. 'I've been thinking of going into the rare stamp market. Larrimore is one of the most important philatelists in the world. I would be so happy to have him as my adviser.'

Elliot stared at him as if he couldn't believe what he was saying.

'Larrimore? Your adviser? Come on, Claude, you're nuts! Not a hope ...'

'Like that?' Kendrick shook his head sadly. 'Well, I must take it you would know.' A pause, then he went on, 'Tell me how you got friendly with Larrimore.'

'Apart from collecting stamps, he is a golfer. Not good, but like most golfers who aren't good, deadly keen. He comes to the club once a week and I play with him from time to time. I cured him of a hell of a slice and since then he has always been friendly. That's it. I don't see anything of him now ... my tin foot fixed my golf.'

'How odd. A slice? Odd how things happen.' Kendrick finished his whisky. 'Although you haven't seen him lately, you could still call on him?'

'Look, Claude, I said forget it,' Elliot said impatiently. 'Larrimore wouldn't help you.' He moved to the door. 'Louis will come tomorrow at ten?'

'Yes.' Kendrick smiled. 'Don't worry too much, cheri. It's always darkest before the dawn.'

'I seem to have heard that somewhere before,' Elliot said and left.

*   *   *

'Well now, Mr Campbell,' Barney said, 'I want you to appreciate how I bring the threads of my story together like weaving a carpet. It's only because I can't spell and my writing isn't so hot that I'm not in your racket. I've got the technique, but the rest is strictly for the gulls.'

I said all of us couldn't aspire to the heights and would he like another hamburger?

'That mightn't be a bad idea,' Barney said and wig-wagged with his eyebrows to Sam. 'Feed the body – feed the mind, huh?'

I said that was an accepted fact.

'Well now ... I've got Joey, Cindy, Vin, Elliot and Kendrick on the stage. Now comes the time to join them together and I'll do it step by step.' Barney waited until Sam produced the hamburger and having inspected it, he nodded approval, then continued, 'Joey couldn't afford to let Cindy stick around making cow's eyes at Vin now he knew Vin was running short of money. As his own ready cash was also getting low, he sent Cindy out to work the stores in the morning instead of the afternoon and he went out also to work the buses, leaving Vin to sit at home, dreaming about the Big Take.

'It so happened that Cindy was walking down the main street, heading for one of the stores when she saw Elliot's Rolls parked by the kerb. The sight of his car brought her to a standstill. Most people paused to stare at the car, but it mesmerized Cindy. This was the car of her dreams and she was standing there, in a white sweatshirt and these things they call "hot pants", worshipping the car when Elliot came out of Kendrick's gallery.

'The first thing Elliot noticed was Cindy's long beautiful legs and then her little bottom and then her tits. These three feminine features had a big attraction for Elliot and for the moment he forgot his worries and even his tin foot. Seeing Cindy gaping at his car, he joined her and said in his screen voice that used to send shivers up and down the spines of his women fans, "She's as lovely as you, isn't she?"

'Cindy spun round, embarrassed, then she laughed.

' "Better! Man! What a gorgeous car!" Then she did a double take as she recognized Elliot.

'Cindy was an Elliot fan. When she was younger, she had adored Errol Flynn. When he passed on, she turned her adoration on Elliot. To find herself standing right by her favourite movie star completely threw her. She clasped her hands and stared, looking a cross between a sheep and a cow as she exclaimed, "It's Don Elliot!"

'Elliot hadn't seen that soppy look for a long time and he reacted to it.

' "Hello," he said and he gave out with his sexy smile which he hadn't used since he had lost his foot. "You know me, but I don't know you. Who are you?"

'Cindy recovered herself.

' "I'm not important, Mr Elliot. I was just passing and I saw this lovely car and I stopped and then you appeared."

' "It's mine," Elliot said, and for the first time he felt this huge bad debt was worth the worry it was giving him. "Would you like a ride?"

' "Would you be kidding, Mr Elliot?"

'Elliot laughed, opened the off-side door and waved her to get in.

'With a dazed expression, Cindy settled herself in the passenger's seat, clasping her hands over her breasts. Elliot drove slowly through the heavy traffic, saying nothing. One quick look at this girl's face told him to let her alone, let her have her dream, let her give herself up to the silent movement of the car. Once clear of the traffic and on to

Seaview Boulevard, he accelerated a little and headed for
the hills. He drove at an easy speed until he reached a long
stretch of deserted road, then he shoved down the gas pedal
and let Cindy experience the sudden rush of silent power
that swept them along at over a hundred miles an hour. As
the road came to an end to join up with the highway to
Miami, he slowed and pulled into a lay-by.

' "What do you think?" he asked. "Maybe you would
like to drive her before you decide."

'Cindy stared at him. She was still a little dazed by the
rush of speed.

' "Decide? What about?"

' "Aren't you going to buy her?" Elliot asked and
grinned. "This was a trial run, wasn't it?"

' "Was it?" She heaved a sigh. "I wish it was. I wish I had
the money. I wish it was mine."

'There was something about Cindy that got to Elliot. He
was so used to dollies who knew everything, never were
impressed, were so ready to get into his bed that Cindy
scored with him.

' "Who are you?" he asked as he lit a cigarette.

'This was something Cindy wasn't going to tell him.

' "Cindy Luck," she told him. "Nobody ... just a girl
getting by."

' "And how do you get by?"

' "You know ... an office ... a typewriter and me."

' "Cindy ... a nice name. Are you lucky?"

' "Oh, yes! To be in this car? Oh, yes!"

'He laughed.

' "Seen any of my movies?"

' "Every one of them! They're like you ... marvellous!"

'No gush here, Elliot thought. This was straight from
the heart.

44

' "Are you on vacation?" '

' "That's right." '

' "On your own?" '

' "I'm with my father." '

'Elliot looked at his wrist watch.

' "I'm hungry. Will you lunch with me or is your father expecting you?" '

'Joey and Vin were, of course, expecting her, but she didn't hesitate. There was half a cold chicken in the refrig and they could manage without her.

' "I'd love to." '

'He took her to his villa.'

*   *   *

Barney began to attack the second tier of his hamburger.

'I want to keep this story moving along, Mr Campbell,' he said, his mouth full. 'There are bits I can skip, but there are bits I have to fill in … to give you the atmosphere so don't think I'm talking for the sake of talking.'

I said for him to go right on ahead.

He nodded.

'Well, Elliot's villa made a tremendous impact on Cindy. She just couldn't believe anyone could live in such luxury. They had lunch on the terrace, overlooking the harbour and the sea, surrounded with banks of flowering shrubs and orchid trees. The lunch was as impeccable as the service: baby shrimps, peppered and served hot, sole fillets in a cheese sauce and iced passion fruit. There was champagne that made Cindy a little light headed.

'Because she was so intrigued with everything she saw, Elliot took her over the villa. She walked by his side, her hands clasped, her eyes round, her breathing fast and uneven. Everything she saw thrilled her.

45

'When he finally brought her back to the living-room she said the nicest thing anyone had ever said to him.

' "It's the loveliest house I have ever seen," she said, "and you deserve it because you have given so much happiness and pleasure to so many people."

'Looking at her, savouring her beauty, Elliot had a surge of desire for her he hadn't had in months. He wanted to lead her into his bedroom, undress her gently and lay her on the bed. He wanted to take her as only he knew how to take a woman, slowly, spreading the pleasure, until the climax came.

'Just for the moment, he felt sure she would give herself to him, then he remembered his tin foot and his desire turned to sourness.

'And while he stood looking at her, his desire leaving him, the nagging, grinding pain in a foot that was ashes in the furnace of an expensive clinic started up.

'All he now wanted was to be rid of her. It had been a happy few hours, now the pain was back and also his worries.

' "Your father will be wondering where you've got to," he said, his voice suddenly curt. "I'll get my man to drive you back."

'Startled by this sudden change in him and a little deflated, Cindy began to thank him, but he waved her thanks away.

' "It's been my pleasure," he said. "Toyo won't be a moment. You must excuse me ... I have things to do. So long for now," and he left her. The three hours she had spent with him were suddenly spoilt by this abrupt dismissal. She felt as if a pail of cold water had been thrown over her.

'The Jap chauffeur drove her back to Seaview Boulevard in the Alfa. She wouldn't let him take her direct to the bungalow. Cindy also resented not being driven back in the

Rolls. She just couldn't understand what had gone wrong – all she knew was that something had gone wrong.'

Barney sipped his beer and then chased with his finger a piece of meat that had got lodged in a tooth.

'She found Vin in the garden. Joey had gone out to work the buses.

' "Where the hell have you been?" Vin demanded. "What happened to you?"

'Cindy told him. As she talked, describing the Rolls and the villa a sudden idea dropped into Vin's mind.

' "This guy must be loaded," he said.

' "Of course. He's a great movie star. Mustn't it be wonderful to have all that money and to live like that?" Cindy sighed. "And that Rolls!"

' "Yeah." Vin's eyes narrowed. "I wonder how much he's worth?"

' "Millions. You couldn't possibly live like that without being worth millions."

' "Are you seeing him again?"

' "No ... he suddenly acted strange." Cindy went on to tell Vin how she and Elliot had parted.

' "Most movie stars are crazy in the head," Vin said. "Didn't he try to make a pass at you?"

'Cindy flushed.

' "Of course, he didn't!"

' "What's the matter with him?" Vin asked. "What did he want to give you a ride for and a meal?"

' "Not everyone thinks the way you do!" Cindy said sharply and went into the bungalow.

'Soon after 17.00 Joey got back from work. He hadn't had much success and he was a little worried. He had stolen five billfolds and the complete take had amounted to forty dollars.

' "Where's Cindy?" he asked, sitting in a deckchair by Vin's side. He removed his hat and mopped his brow. "Did she get anything? I only got forty bucks."

' "She's washing her hair or some damn thing," Vin said. "Yes, she got something. Joey! I think this is the big take!"

'Joey stiffened and stared at him.

' "Big take? What do you mean?"

' "You remember I said I wanted to find a job worth fifty thousand bucks and then we would leave here, buy a bungalow somewhere up the coast and we three would settle down and I'd marry Cindy?"

'Joey looked fearfully at Vin.

' "Yes ... but that was all talk, wasn't it?"

' "We three are going to pick up fifty grand," Vin said, his eyes glittering. "It'll be like taking a nickel off a blind man."

' "But how?" Joey asked, his heart beginning to pound.

'Fifty thousand dollars! he thought. This was the big league – something he had always been careful to avoid.

' "Take it easy and listen," Vin said. He went on to tell Joey about Cindy's meeting with Don Elliot. "You remember the guy? One time he was top in the movies. Cindy says he's loaded. He runs a Rolls. That alone must have set him back $30,000. His villa is stuffed with good loot."

'Joey licked his dry lips.

' "Are you thinking of knocking over his place?"

' "Don't talk wet!" Vin snapped. "Who would take the loot? Besides, I'd have to have a truck to move stuff worth all that money. No, Joey, we're going to snatch this guy and we're going to hold him to ransom!"

'Joey nearly jumped out of his chair.

' "Oh, no! They can put you in the gas chamber for kidnapping!" Joey's eyes grew round with terror. "Not me ... not Cindy! Kidnapping's out!"

' "This isn't kidnapping," Vin said impatiently. "We capture the guy and tell him we want fifty thousand bucks. What's fifty grand to him … peanuts! We keep him until he pays up. No one will even know we have got him. I've got all this worked out."

' "No!" Joey got to his feet. He was so agitated he began to shake. "I don't care what you call it. This is out!"

'Vin looked contemptuously at him, then shrugged.

' "Okay, Joey, if that's the way you feel about it. We can swing this without you. I can even swing it without Cindy. When I get the dough Cindy and I will leave you. It's as simple as that."

' "Cindy won't have anything to do with this!" Joey said. "She won't touch it!"

' "Here she comes. Let's ask her," Vin said as Cindy came across the small lawn and joined them.

' "Ask me what?" she asked. "What's the matter, dad? You look worked up."

' "He's planning to kidnap this movie star!" Joey said. "He's crazy! I told him you wouldn't have anything to do with it!"

'Cindy looked quickly at Vin.

' "Kidnap? Oh, Vin!"

' "So what?" Vin stretched out his long legs. "We don't hurt the guy. He's loaded. All we do is to keep him here under lock and key until he parts with fifty grand. There's nothing to it. When we get the dough we three will go up the coast; you and me will get married and we'll settle down to three years or so without doing a thing. What do you say, baby? You with me?"

'Cindy stared first at Vin and then at Joey, then back to Vin again.

' "You must be crazy, Vin," she said. "No ... I'm not doing it!"

' "There's nothing crazy about it," Vin said, trying to control his impatience. "You said this guy is loaded. Okay, so what's fifty grand to him? He'll pay. There's nothing to it. Just imagine we three with fifty grand!"

'Cindy hesitated. If Elliot hadn't dismissed her in the way he had, she wouldn't have hesitated, but now, thinking what fifty thousand dollars could mean to them all, she did hesitate.

' "But suppose he won't pay?"

'Joey stiffened.

' "Cindy! Listen to me ..." Then he stopped because he saw she wasn't listening.

' "You want to marry me, don't you?" Vin said. "You want some fun? This way we can do what you want. Come on, Cindy, say you'll go along with me."

'Cindy was sick of the way she and Joey had been living. She had never complained, but this small way of life after meeting Vin was becoming unbearable. She thought again of what all that money could mean to them and she made her decision.

' "Yes, Vin. I'll help you."

'Vin looked at Joey.

' "Looks like the majority has it, Joey. Do you want to come in or do you want to split up?"

' "Cindy." Joey put his hand on Cindy's arm. "This is dangerous. It's kidnapping. We'll be up against the Feds. We could go away for life. We could even go to the gas chamber. You mustn't do this, baby."

' "Fifty grand," Vin said softly. "No more dipping. No more taking risks in a self-service store. A nice little home ... and me, but suit yourself, Cindy. I'm going to pull it with you and Joey, or without you and Joey ... please yourself."

50

' "I said I'll do it, Vin," Cindy said quietly.

'Vin looked at Joey.

' "Going to change your mind or do we split up?"

' "You really think it'll work?" Joey said weakly.

' "You think I'm nuts? Of course it will work."

'Joey hesitated. Looking at the determined expression on Cindy's face he knew he couldn't persuade her not to go ahead. He saw there was nothing else for him to do but to throw in with Vin. He wasn't to lose Cindy.

' "Okay, Vin ... count me in," he said.'

3

The following morning, Barney told me, Elliot sat on his patio in the sun waiting with impatience for Louis de Marney to complete the inventory of his possessions.

Finally, Louis came out on to the patio and Elliot, controlling his eagerness to know the verdict, offered him a drink.

'Absolutely not, thank you. No drinks ... no starch! I would never keep my figure if I relaxed for a moment.' Louis eyed Elliot. 'Yet you keep in beautiful form.'

Elliot, naked to the waist, wearing a pair of slacks, socks and sandals, shrugged. He hated wearing socks, but without them the glitter of his tin foot in the sun depressed him.

'I guess I'm okay. Sit down.' He paused, then went on. 'Well, what's the verdict?'

'You have some very nice things, Mr Elliot,' Louis said, sitting down, 'a little specialized, but very nice.'

'I know what I've got,' Elliot said impatiently. 'What I want to know is what the lot's worth.'

'Of course.' Louis waved his hands. 'I can't give you a definite figure, Mr Elliot. You understand I will have to consult Claude, but I'd say around seventy-five thousand.'

Elliot stiffened and flushed. He hadn't expected Louis to be generous but this figure was daylight robbery.

'Are you kidding?' he demanded angrily. 'That's less than a quarter of what I originally paid!'

Louis looked sad. 'It does sound dreadful, doesn't it? Right now, Mr Elliot, it just isn't a buyer's market. If you could wait ...' He chewed his under lip, frowning while he appeared to think. 'Claude might agree to take the jade and the Chagall on a commission basis and display them in the gallery. That way you could get a better price, but it would, of course, take time.'

'How much better?'

'That I can't tell you. Claude would have to decide the price.'

'How long would I have to wait ... two or three months?'

Louis shook his head. He looked as if he could burst into tears.

'Oh no, Mr Elliot, it could be as long as two years. You see jade ... but I'm sure jade will come back into fashion and again fetch high prices, but not for a year or two.'

Elliot thumped his knee with his fist.

'I can't wait that long! Claude can afford to wait! Talk to him, Louis. Tell him he can have the jade and the Chagall but I want immediate cash and a decent price ... not a crappy offer of seventy-five thousand!'

Louis studied his beautifully manicured fingernails.

'Of course I will talk to him.' A pause, then he went on, 'Claude did mention to me that you wanted quick cash, Mr Elliot. All this is strictly between you, Claude and myself. We could offer you an interesting proposition since you need money badly. This would be interesting money: something like two hundred thousand. That, plus seventy-five for your things would give you a sum that would make life much happier for you.'

Elliot stared at him.

'Two hundred thousand?' He sat up. 'What is this interesting proposition?'

53

'You are a friend of Mr Larrimore, the philatelist?'

Elliot's eyes narrowed.

'Is this proposition to do with Larrimore?'

Louis looked at Elliot, then the little eyes shifted. 'That's right.'

'Claude and I have already talked about Larrimore. I told him he hadn't a hope.'

'Claude's thinking has developed further since you talked to him,' Louis said like a man feeling his way across thin ice. 'He is now ready to offer you two hundred thousand for your co-operation.'

Elliot drew in a deep breath. He thought what this kind of money could mean to him in his present situation.

'My co-operation? Look, Louis, will you stop talking like a goddamn politician and explain what you're getting at?'

'Mr Larrimore has some specialized Russian stamps,' Louis said shifting his eyes back to his fingernails. 'Claude has a client who wants to buy them. We have already written to Mr Larrimore offering to buy these stamps, but he ignores our letters. If you could get these stamps for us, Claude would pay you a commission of two hundred thousand.'

'For God's sake! How much are they worth?'

'To you or to me ... very little, but to a keen collector a great deal.'

'How much?'

'I don't think we need go into that, Mr Elliot.' Louis gave Elliot a foxy smile. 'The point we are discussing is that these stamps if you can get them would be worth two hundred thousand to you.'

Elliot sat back. This could be the way to solve his present problems, he thought, but could he persuade Larrimore to sell?

'If I'm going to talk to Larrimore I must have a figure,' he said. 'That's obvious, isn't it? I have to tell him the sum your man wants to pay. How else can I persuade him to sell?'

Louis ran his fingers through his sable tinted hair.

'I don't think you would get anywhere with Mr Larrimore whatever sum you offered. Our client has already written to him and Mr Larrimore won't sell. No, approaching Mr Larrimore would only end in disaster.'

Elliot frowned. 'So just what are you getting at?'

Louis again studied his fingernails as if he found them fascinating.

'We felt that as you are on friendly terms with Mr Larrimore and have access to his house, you might see a way to get hold of these stamps. If you did, we would pay you immediately two hundred thousand in cash.' Louis got to his feet as Elliot stared at him as if he didn't believe what he was hearing. 'And, of course, there would be no questions asked.'

Elliot remained still for a long moment, then he said, a grating note in his voice, 'Are you suggesting I should steal these stamps for Claude?'

Louis waved his hands, not looking at Elliot.

'We're not suggesting anything, Mr Elliot. You happen to have the opportunity of getting the stamps – how you get them is no business of ours – we will accept them from you, ask no questions and give you two hundred thousand dollars.'

Elliot got to his feet. The look in his eyes made Louis take a hurried step back.

'Get out!' The anger in Elliot's voice made Louis retreat still further. 'Tell Claude I don't deal with crooks! I'll find someone to buy my stuff! Tell him he's seen the last of me!'

Louis lifted his shoulders in a resigned shrug.

'I did warn him you might not go along with his thinking, but Claude is a complete optimist. No hard feelings, Mr Elliot. Of course the offer stands should you change your mind.'

'Get out!'

Louis sighed and turning, he weaved his way down the path that led to the car park. He drove back to the gallery and went immediately to Claude's room.

'The sonofabitch won't play,' he said as he shut the door. 'He called you a crook and said he never wanted to see you again. I warned you, Claude. Now what are we going to do?'

Kendrick took off his wig and laid it on the desk while he thought.

'It was a chance and it still could remain a good chance. I will bring a little pressure to bear on dear Don.' He brooded, then opening his desk drawer he took from it a leather bound address book. 'Who would you say is Elliot's biggest creditor?'

'Luce & Fremlin.' Louis said promptly. 'He has given every tramp he's laid a piece of jewellery. The last one got a diamond and ruby ring that must have cost the earth.'

Kendrick consulted his book, then called Luce & Fremlin, the best and most expensive jewellers in the City.

He asked to be connected with Mr Fremlin, the junior partner and a raving homosexual.

'Sydney, my beautiful poinciana, this is your devoted Claude. How am I? Oh, pretty fair, struggling to make both ends meet.' He giggled. 'And you? So glad.' A pause. 'Sydney, a word in your ear. I don't know if Don Elliot owes you anything – yes, the ex-movie star. He does? I thought he just might. I'm worried about him. He owes me too. I sent Louis to talk to him this morning. You know how tactful I am. Louis tried to get a cheque from him, but Elliot turned rather nasty. We get the impression here that he isn't in the position to pay. Dreadful, isn't it? Of course the poor fellow is now handicapped without his foot and without film work, but I did imagine he was financially sound. Does he owe you much?' Claude listened, then lifted his eyebrows and released a soft whistle. 'My poor darling! Fifty thousand! But that's a fortune! I'm only in the hole for five.' He listened again. 'Well, I would act fast if I were you. I can't imagine he is going to be worth much now. He hasn't had a girl since he lost his foot. Terribly, terribly sad. I thought I would alert you. Yes, do let's meet sometime. Bye now.'

As he hung up, Louis said, 'That should get things moving.'

'Poor Sydney ... rather foolish, but I like him. Well, let's not waste time. Elliot's booze, catering and tailor's bills must be impressive.' Kendrick replaced his wig. 'Perhaps a word in those dears' ears might be a charitable act,' and he reached again for the telephone receiver.

*　　*　　*

Toyo, Elliot's chauffeur, met Winston Ackland at the Paradise City airport and drove him to Elliot's villa. Ackland had arrived in his own light aircraft, flying from Miami at Elliot's urgent request.

Ackland was short, fat and full of bustle. He was one of the leading antique and art experts in Miami with a flourishing gallery and was always on the look-out for a bargain. When Elliot had told him he had a Chagall he wanted to sell and a collection of jade, Ackland said he would be over that afternoon.

Elliot watched him as he examined the Chagall. The expression on Ackland's fat face told him nothing. Finally Ackland turned away from the painting.

'This could be an Emile Houry, but it is certainly not a Chagall,' he said. 'A nice fake. I hope it didn't cost you too much, Mr Elliot.'

'A hundred thousand,' Elliot said, his voice husky. 'Are you sure it's a fake?'

'You can never be entirely sure, but that's my opinion,' Ackland said quietly. 'I suppose Kendrick sold it to you?'

'Yes.'

'Kendrick isn't as good with this kind of art as he thinks he is,' Ackland said. 'He could have been deceived. Even some of the top experts have been deceived by Houty, but I happen to specialize in Chagall and I'm sure this isn't one of his ... at least almost sure.'

Elliot felt cold sweat break out on his forehead.

'And the jade ... don't tell me that's a fake too.'

'Oh no. That's a very nice collection. I would offer you twenty thousand for it.'

'Can you give me anything for the Chagall?'

Ackland shook his head. 'I don't want it. It's a painting that could get any dealer into trouble.'

'And the rest?'

'Nothing impressive, but if you want to get rid of all the paintings, I would offer ten thousand. I'm sorry to offer so little, but these paintings are just decorations ... they have no value.'

Elliot hesitated, then shrugged.

'Okay ... give me a note for thirty thousand to be paid in cash and the stuff's yours.'

Ackland gave him the note. When he had gone, Elliot did some thinking. Maybe, he thought, Claude didn't know the Chagall was a fake. He hesitated for a long moment, then he rang Kendrick's gallery.

Louis answered.

'Give me Claude,' Elliot said.

'It's Mr Elliot?'

'Yeah.'

'A tiny moment.'

Then Kendrick came on the line.

'If you want the Chagall you can have it,' Elliot said.

'My dear boy ... what a nice surprise. From what Louis told me you were cross with me,' Kendrick said, startled to get this call.

'Never mind that. What will you give me for the Chagall before I offer it to Winston Ackland?'

'Ackland? You mustn't do that, dear boy! He would give you absolutely nothing! He'd probably tell you it's a fake. Ackland is really rather horrid.'

'What do you offer?'

'I would rather take it on commission, dear Don. I could get you ...'

'I want cash ... remember? How much?'

'Thirty thousand.'

'I paid a hundred thousand.'

'I know, but these are dreadful times.'

'You can have it for forty-five: immediate cash.'

'Forty, my dear boy. That's absolute top.'

'Send Louis with your note to be paid in cash and he can take it away,' Elliot said and hung up.

Kendrick replaced the receiver and beamed at Louis.

'The poor stupid dear has sold us the Chagall for forty. Imagine! That silly Mrs Van Johnson is aching for a Chagall. If I don't get a hundred thousand out of her, I'll eat my wig!'

'Watch it, Claude,' Louis said. 'If she has it checked ...'

'Of course she won't have it checked as Elliot didn't have it checked.' Kendrick sat back, his fat face wreathed in smiles. 'My word is their guarantee.'

*　　*　　*

By 15.00 that afternoon, Elliot had seventy thousand dollars in cash. He had cashed Ackland's note and Kendrick's note at another bank, not his own. He knew if he had tried to cash these notes at his own bank the dreary question of his overdraft would have come up.

As he locked the money away in his desk drawer, he felt he had gained breathing space. He could pay his staff and use the rest of the money to continue his way of life for a few more months. For the first time in weeks, he felt relaxed.

Then the telephone bell rang.

Frowning, Elliot snatched up the receiver. The caller was Larry Kaufman, the Rolls Royce agent.

'Mr Elliot?' Kaufman's voice sounded sharp and hostile. 'I'm asking you to settle for the Rolls. My people are pressing me. You've had the car over two months now. They're insisting on immediate settlement.'

Elliot hesitated, but only for a moment. He still had the Alfa which was paid for and he would be out of his mind to part with thirty thousand no matter how much he loved the Rolls. He knew he must now hang on to every dollar he could lay his hands on.

'You can take it back, Larry. I've changed my mind. I don't want it.'

'You don't want it?' Kaufman's voice shot up.

'That's what I said.'

'I can't take it back just like that ... damn it! It's a second hand car now!'

60

'Well, okay, so take it back as a second hand car. What am I bid?'

'You're sure you want to do this, Mr Elliot?'

'What am I bid?'

'I'll give you an honest deal as I can sell the car the moment I have it. Suppose you owe me three thousand?'

'You think that's honest.'

'It is honest and you know it, Mr Elliot.'

'Okay ... okay. Come and get it. I'll have a cheque ready for you.'

Elliot tried to be indifferent about this, but it gave him a pang to see Kaufman drive the Rolls away with a cheque for three thousand in his pocket. Elliot wondered if the cheque would bounce. He hoped his bank manager would extend his overdraft. Anyway, he thought, it was worth a try.

After lunch, as he was settling down on the patio for a nap, his bank manager called.

'Don ... Kaufman has just been in and presented your cheque for three thousand. I've honoured it because you and I are good friends, but this is the last time. You have to do something about this overdraft. No more cheques, Don. Understand?'

'Sure ... sure ... I'll sell some stock,' Elliot said glibly. 'By the end of the week I'll have fixed it.'

The wolves were closing in, he thought. Well, at least he had seventy thousand in cash in his desk drawer. It might be an idea to get in the Alfa and go to Hollywood, stay at a motel for a couple of weeks and let his debts take care of themselves. The more he thought about this, the better he liked the idea, but this wasn't his day. As he got up with the intention of packing a bag and getting out, his major domo came out on to the patio.

'There's a gentleman ...'

61

A tall, hard faced man, carrying a briefcase, stepped around the major domo and came up to Elliot.

'I'm Stan Jerrold, Mr Elliot.' He paused until the major domo had left them, then went on. 'I've been briefed by Luce & Fremlin and Handcock & Ellison to collect two outstanding debts. I've been instructed to issue you with a summons to be returned at the Courthouse at the end of the month if I don't get a certified cheque right now.'

'Is that right?' Elliot forced a grin. Once a summons was issued all the wolves would rush in. 'How much is it for?'

'Sixty-one thousand dollars.'

This jolted Elliot but he managed to retain his grin.

'As much as that?' He knew he couldn't afford to be served with a summons. 'I'll give you cash.'

Ten minutes later, Jerrold left, his briefcase bulging, and Elliot's cash assets had abruptly shrunk to nine thousand dollars.

He lit a cigarette and leaning back in his desk chair, he considered his future. It looked bleaker than ever before. He knew the word would get around that he was paying his debts. In a day or so his other creditors would come knocking on his door. It was time to get out and get out fast. He would drive to Hollywood and when his nine thousand dollars had run out, he would take enough sleeping pills to make headlines for the last time.

Going into his bedroom, he packed a suitcase, selecting the best of his wardrobe, conscious that none of the clothes he was putting into the suitcase had been paid for. He included a bottle of Scotch and a carton of two hundred cigarettes.

He took three hundred dollars from his diminishing roll and went in search of his major domo. Finding him in the kitchen, he explained he was going away and gave him the money. 'This should hold you until I get back. I'm going to see Mr Lewishon.'

The major domo bowed and gave Elliot a sad, searching stare as he took the money. The stare told Elliot the old man was aware of the mess he was in.

'I'll write if I stay away longer than a week,' Elliot said, uncomfortable at the searching stare and the sadness on the old man's face. He returned to his bedroom, paused to look around, feeling sure this would be the last time he would call this room his own. Then shrugging, he picked up the suitcase and walked down to the garage.

As he was getting into the Alfa Romeo, he saw a girl walking slowly up the drive: a blonde, wearing a white sweatshirt and scarlet shorts,

'Cindy Luck!' he thought, surprised and he drove down, pulling up beside her. 'Hello.' He smiled. 'What brings you here?'

Cindy seemed ill at ease and her smile forced.

'I – I wanted to see you again.'

Vin, Joey and she had gone over the kidnap plan. Vin felt sure that Cindy could get Elliot to their bungalow.

'Get him here,' he said, 'then I'll handle him.'

Cindy had hesitated.

'You won't hurt him, Vin?'

'Hurt him? Forget it! I'll just poke a gun at him and he'll fall to pieces. I know these phoney tough guys. They're fine up there on the screen, but show them a gun in real life and they're just wet spaghetti.'

Elliot regarded her. 'She's certainly a dish,' he thought. 'If it wasn't for this goddamn tin foot, I'd get her laid.'

'Well, here I am,' he said. 'I'm just off to Hollywood.'

Cindy's eyes opened wide. This was unexpected.

'Oh, Mr Elliot! My father will be so disappointed. He is a terrific fan of yours. When I told him I had been here and you had actually given me lunch – honest, he nearly died with envy. He was really upset so I said I would try to persuade you to come and see him.' Her mind worked swiftly as she saw alarm come into Elliot's eyes. 'I know it's asking a lot but my father is an invalid and he has so little pleasure. He's seen all your movies and he really thinks you're the greatest ... as I do.'

Elliot hesitated, then thought: 'What have I got to lose? I now haven't a friend in the world and here's this kid ... what a dish! It won't kill me to see her old man. It'll give them both a hell of a kick.' He smiled. 'Okay. Where do you live, Cindy?'

'On Seaview Boulevard.'

'That's fine. It's in my direction. Hop in.' Elliot leaned over and opened the offside door. 'I can't stay long, but if it will please your old man, it's my pleasure.'

Cindy felt suddenly sick. She had allowed herself to be persuaded by Vin to take part in this kidnap plan. As Vin pointed out the money would mean nothing to Elliot and once they had got it, they would get married and have a ball. She had gone along with this, not thinking of Elliot, but now he was being so kind, she began to have qualms. For a long moment, she stood hesitating, then when he told her to hurry up, she obeyed and got in the car.

'I can't thank you enough,' she said, not looking at him. 'You don't know what this will mean to my father.'

'Forget it,' Elliot said as he drove on to the highway. 'I'm repaying a little debt. You said something very nice to me – something no one has ever said to me.'

'Did I?'

'You wouldn't remember because it came from your heart. You were talking about my home. You said I deserved it because I had given so much pleasure to so many people.' He smiled at her. 'I'm now trying to live up to your image of me.'

Cindy looked away. For a brief moment, she was on the point of telling him she was leading him into a trap, but thinking of Vin and her father and how much this money would mean to them and that this nice movie star wouldn't miss giving them fifty thousand dollars when he must be worth millions, she resisted the urge.

'Thank you,' she said. 'I did mean what I said and you are living up to my image.'

Elliot drove fast to Seaview Boulevard. He was a little puzzled that this girl at his side seemed so tense. As she remained silent, he asked abruptly, 'Anything on your mind, baby? Something wrong?'

Cindy stiffened.

'Wrong? No. I was thinking how lucky I am and how kind you are.'

Elliot laughed. 'Oh, come on, Cindy! Don't soft soap me. I'm just behaving like a normal human being.'

'Are you?' Cindy thought of Vin and for the first time since she had fallen in love with him, she realized with a little pang that there was no kindness in him. He was hard, tough and glamorous but without kindness and Cindy suddenly realised kindness was as important as glamour. She compared Vin with Elliot and then Elliot with Joey. Elliot and Joey were a lot alike: they had warmth, but not Vin.

'Not many people who are as famous and as rich as you,' she said quietly, 'would bother with people like my father and myself.'

'Wouldn't they?'

65

Maybe she was right, he thought. He wondered if he would have bothered with her if Pacific Pictures had renewed his contract. He decided he wouldn't. He wondered what he was letting himself in for. The old man would probably be a godawful bore. Well, he needn't stay long.

'I'm seeing my agent tomorrow,' he said. 'I could be starting work again.'

Cindy turned. Her face lit up and she looked so pleased Elliot cursed himself for telling such a stupid lie.

'I'm so glad! I read about the accident. It just made me sick. It was so awful for you.'

Elliot shrugged. 'These things happen.' He hesitated, then went on. 'My left foot is made of tin now.' He looked sharply at her. 'That shock you?'

'Shock me? Why should it? You walk beautifully. No one would know.'

'They know when I take my shoe off.' The bitter note in his voice made her flinch.

'Yes ... I understand. I'm sorry.'

'Why should you be sorry?'

She hesitated.

'Well, go on, say it.'

'It must be hard on you. I'm sure you had lots of girls ... you shouldn't let a thing like this spoil your life.' Again she hesitated. 'What has a foot to do with it when a man and a woman are in love?'

Elliot whistled softly between his teeth.

'You don't know, kid. It makes a hell of a difference. You just don't know.'

'I said if a man and a woman are in love. I don't mean just jumping into bed ... I mean love.'

'Would it make any difference to you?'

'I plan to get married very soon,' Cindy said, not looking at him.

'You are?' Elliot was startled that what she had told him gave him a let down feeling. This sudden pang of disappointment irritated him. What was this chick to him? She was a dish, of course, but nothing more and yet to be told she was getting married depressed him. 'Who's the lucky man?'

'You'll meet him. He's staying with father and me.' Cindy pointed. 'It's the end bungalow on the right.'

Elliot surveyed the small bungalow, half hidden by shrubs. He was not surprised by its shabbiness. In fact, he rather liked its down-trodden appearance ... so different from his own luxury home.

He pulled up outside the gate behind Vin's blue Jaguar.

'Is that your boyfriend's car?' he asked as Cindy joined him on the sidewalk.

'Yes.'

'Good cars ... well, come on, chick, I can't stay long.'

Cindy led the way up the path to the front door.

Joey and Vin watched from behind the net curtains. Joey was sweating and his legs felt weak. Vin held a .38 automatic and he was breathing heavily.

'She's done it!' he said. 'I knew she would! Well, here comes fifty grand! Just leave this to me.'

'Don't hurt him,' Joey pleaded. 'Be careful Vin. I don't like any of this. I ...'

'Just shut up, will you?' Vin snarled. 'I'll handle it.'

Cindy opened the front door.

'Please come in.' Her voice was so husky Elliot looked at her. She had lost colour and now looked terrified.

'What's with it, baby?' he asked, puzzled. 'Are you all right?'

Then he heard a sound behind him and he looked around.

Vin stood in the open doorway of the living-room, the gun pointing at Elliot.

'Just take it easy, buster,' Vin said, his voice like a fall of gravel. 'Come on in. One wrong move from you and I'll give you a second belly button.'

For a moment Elliot was startled, then he quickly recovered. He smiled.

'That dialogue is right out of a B movie,' he said, then he looked at Cindy. 'I'm disappointed in you. Who would have thought you would turn out to be a gangster's moll?' He laughed. 'More B movie dialogue.'

* * *

Here, Barney paused. He regarded me with a sly look, then said, 'Would you like to try Sam's sausages, Mr Campbell? They are one of the specialities of the house. They are soaked in rum before being fried in a chilli sauce. I can recommend them.'

I explained that I had had dinner and I had to watch my weight.

'Too much attention is paid to weight watching,' Barney said, a note of scorn in his voice. 'You live only once, mister. I'd hate to think of all the food I might have missed if I watched my weight. You follow my reasoning?'

I said I got the idea and perhaps he would like a sausage or two, but strictly not for me.

He smiled and lifted one thick finger at Sam. This must have been a pre-arranged signal for Sam came hurrying over with a plate of a dozen small sausages, the colour of mahogany, their skins wrinkled and glistening.

'Try one,' Barney said, pushing the plate towards me, but something warned me to resist. I said for him to go ahead and count me out. 'They're hot,' Barney said, feeding one of the sausages into his little mouth. He chewed and I saw his eyes begin to water and I was thankful I had been strong minded. After a long swill of beer, Barney wiped his eyes with the back of his hand and settled himself. 'Real dynamite,' he said, nodding his approval. 'I've seen so-called tough guys jump three feet in the air after just one of these little beauties.'

'You got to this kidnapping,' I said. 'So what happened?'

Barney reached for another sausage as he said, 'Well, Vin acted tough and he could be tough when he was in the mood. He scared the hell out of Cindy and Joey but he made no impact on Elliot.

'Elliot walked into the living-room and sat down in the best armchair. He ignored Vin and the threatening gun and concentrated on Joey. He liked the look of Joey and was surprised to see the old man was trembling.

' "Is this your father, Cindy?" he asked.

' "Yes." Cindy was also trembling.

'Elliot nodded to Joey.

' "I congratulate you. You have a lovely daughter, Mr Luck. And this gentleman waving the gun at me … is he your fiancé?"

' "Now listen, buster," Vin snarled. "Button up! I do the talking around here!"

'Elliot continued to ignore Vin. To Cindy, he said, "I wouldn't have thought he was your style. This act of his wouldn't jell even on TV. I thought you could have aimed higher than him."

'Vin recognized he was being challenged. He saw Cindy's uneasy look and also Joey's reaction.

' "Okay, punk," he said viciously. In the past, he had dealt with tough guys, smart punks and creeps who looked for trouble. This tall, handsome movie star had to be cut down to size and to learn right away who was the boss. Moving forward, he reached out and made a grab at Elliot's shirt front. The idea was to jerk Elliot out of the chair, rush him across the room, slam him against the wall and knock the breath out of him, but it didn't work that way.

'Elliot chopped down on Vin's wrist, lifted his foot and rammed it into Vin's chest to send him flying over him and the chair to crash on an occasional table, flattening it, the gun falling out of his hand.

'Elliot was on his feet and had caught up the gun while Vin lay still, stunned.

' "I'm sorry, Mr Luck," Elliot said mildly. "I hope that table isn't valuable."

'Joey stood speechless, aware that Elliot was holding the gun. Into his mind came a vision of a patrol car pulling up and Cindy and he being bundled into it and the iron gates of a prison clanging behind them for at least ten years.

'Why had he listened to Vin? Why hadn't he insisted that Cindy should have had nothing to do with this thing?

'Cindy, backed against the wall, looked with terrified eyes at Vin, wondering if he was badly hurt.

' "Don't look so upset," Elliot said to her. "He's all right. What's a little tumble to a he-man like him?"

'Vin shook his head, trying to clear it. Then he got unsteadily to his feet. He glared at Elliot, his mouth working with rage, his fists clenched.

' "Make a wrong move, buster," Elliot said with a grin, "and I'll give you a second belly button."

'Looking at Vin with his viciousness and then at Elliot, calm, amused and completely unflustered, Cindy felt a sudden change of heart. She realized that Vin wasn't the man for her. The realisation came as a shock to her and she moved quickly to Joey and caught hold of his hand. Joey, who sensed things, knew with frightened joy that he had got his daughter back.

' "Suppose we all sit down and talk this thing over," Elliot said. "You over there." He waved Vin to a chair by the window, some ten feet from where he was standing. "Go on ... sit down unless you want me to let this heater off and get the police here."

'Muttering, but cowed, Vin went to the chair and sat down. Elliot smiled at Cindy.

' "You and dad sit there, please," and he waved to the sofa.

'Glad to sit down, Joey went to the sofa and he and Cindy sat side by side.

'Elliot took a chair away from them all. He put the gun on the arm of the chair, took out a pack of cigarettes and watching Vin, he lit the cigarette.

' "Well now, Cindy. You owe me an explanation. What's all this about?"

'Joey squeezed Cindy's arm.

' "Tell him, baby," he said. "The truth never hurts anyone."

' "Oh, shut up!" Vin snarled. "Keep your mouth shut, Cindy! Don't listen to him!"

'Cindy flushed and her eyes snapped. No man talked that way to her and got away with it.

' "Mr Elliot ... I'm so ashamed," she said, looking straight at Elliot. "It seemed so easy ... we want money terribly badly. It was Vin's idea. When he heard I'd met you, he said it would be easy to kidnap you and you'd pay to be freed. It didn't sound bad the way Vin put it. He promised not to hurt you. As you are so rich, my father and I felt you wouldn't miss the ransom and we could make a new life for ourselves. Now, of course, I see how wrong it was. Please forgive us."

71

'Elliot gaped at her.

' "Ransom? What were you going to ask?"

'Cindy looked at Joey for guidance and Joey nodded.

' "Fifty thousand dollars. With all your money, Mr Elliot ... you wouldn't have missed that, would you?"

'Elliot burst out laughing. While Joey and Cindy stared at him and Vin glared savagely, Elliot laughed until he had to mop his eyes with his handkerchief.

' "What's so funny about it?" Cindy asked nervously.

' "Funny? It's the best joke of the year! My poor, misguided people, I bet I'm as broke as you are. All I have in the world is my car, a suitcase of clothes and nine thousand dollars in cash – and the money don't belong to me. I'm getting out of here before my creditors catch up with me. You certainly picked the wrong victim. What's the matter with you three? Didn't you ask around? Don't you know you should never take anyone on face value?"

' "He's bluffing," Vin said and tried to get out of his chair.

'Elliot dropped his hand on the gun.

' "I wouldn't, pal," he said. "Even with a tin foot I can handle you." There was a look in his eyes that made Vin sink back in the chair.

' "You mean you really haven't any money ... you're not rich?" Cindy asked. "But the Rolls and that marvellous villa! You can't expect us to believe that!"

' "The Rolls went back to the agent a few hours ago. The villa doesn't belong to me. I'm on the run, baby, I'm washed up."

' "Yeah? No one's washed up with nine thousand dollars," Vin said.

' "How long will that last? When it's gone ... that's it. I've no way of making a living. I'm through."

' "But all that money... you could live on it for at least two years," Cindy said, thinking how little they managed to live on.

' "Lots of people could live on it for years, but not me," Elliot said. "I either keep my standards or I don't want to go on living."

'There was a pause, then Joey, speaking for the first time, said, "I don't think that's right thinking, Mr Elliot, if you'll excuse me saying so. We live on two hundred dollars a week and we get by."

' "I don't want to get by," Elliot said. "I want to live. If you were so satisfied living on two hundred a week why stick your neck out on a kidnapping rap?"

'Joey flinched.

' "I didn't want to do it," he said earnestly. "I wouldn't have done it, Mr Elliot."

' "He's right," Cindy said. "Vin and I persuaded him. We want money! I'm sick of living like this! I'm sick of stealing every day. I want a big sum of money so I can enjoy myself and not go out dipping into people's pockets."

'Elliot lifted his eyebrows.

' "Is that what you do?"

' "Yes! Daddy does the same! Every day! And all we get out of it is a mingy two hundred a week."

' "And what does he do apart from waving guns at people?" Elliot asked, nodding towards Vin.

' "That's my business!" Vin barked. "You keep your mouth shut, Cindy! You're talking too much!"

' "He's a burglar," Cindy said, ignoring Vin.

' "An interesting trio." Elliot smiled at them. "I'm sorry I can't help you. In my better days, I might have been tempted to give you fifty thousand, but you've arrived a little late." He got to his feet. "I must be on my way." He left the gun on the arm of the chair and moved to the door.

"Take my tip ... lay off the kidnapping racket. I don't think you're in that league."

' "You're right, Mr Elliot," Joey said. He paused, hesitated, then blurted out, "You're not planning to make trouble for us? I mean ... the police?"

' "Of course not," Elliot said. "Who knows? In a little while the police may come looking for me." He had said this jokingly but the truth of it suddenly struck him. He realized with a sense of shock that he was no better than these three professional thieves. They stole in a small way, but he had been stealing in a big way. By walking out like this he was stealing from the bank and his creditors. The nine thousand dollars in his hip pocket was stolen. The clothes on his back and in his suitcase were stolen. "Goddamn it," he thought. "I'm a thief. I'm as dishonest as these three are!" Then into his mind came the memory of Louis de Marney as he said, "You have the opportunity of getting the stamps – how you get them is no business of ours – we will accept them from you, ask no questions and give you two hundred thousand."

'Elliot studied the three as they sat looking at him. Maybe with their help, he could get hold of these stamps. Suppose he paid them fifty thousand? That would leave him with a hundred and fifty. With that kind of money he could really have a ball before he called it a day.

'The idea caught fire in his mind.

' "If you three really want fifty thousand," he said, "how about earning it?" He came back to his chair and sat down.

' "How would you like to do a job with me?"

'Vin eyed him suspiciously.

' "What kind of job?"

' "In your line." Leaning forward, Elliot told them about the Russian stamps.'

4

As Louis de Marney was winding down the steel grille that protected the window of the gallery, he saw Elliot coming down the street from the parking lot. He nipped into Kendrick's room to warn him.

Kendrick, who was preparing to go home, smiled his oily smile.

'I was rather expecting him. Show him in, cheri, and stick around. I might just need you.'

As Louis returned to the gallery, Elliot opened the door and entered.

'Why, Mr Elliot! How nice!' Louis gushed. 'Did you want a little *mot* with Claude?'

'Yeah.' Elliot's eyes were hard and his face tense. 'He hasn't gone yet?'

'Just on the very point, but I know he'll see you. You go right on ahead, Mr Elliot.'

Elliot found Kendrick pouring himself a whisky.

'My dear Don! What a nice surprise! Have some of this poison with me? It's so bad to drink alone and Louis, the stupid dear, has given it up. All he thinks about is his figure.'

'Thanks.' Elliot closed the door, went over to a chair and sat down.

Kendrick brought his drink, set it on a side table, then went behind his desk, folding his bulk into his chair.

'What's brought you here, cheri?'

Elliot lit a cigarette.

'Tell me about these Russian stamps you're interested in, Claude.'

'If you can get them, Donny boy, I will ...'

'I know all that. Louis made it clear. Let's have the dope about them and don't, for God's sake, call me Donny boy!'

'So sorry ... a slip of the tongue.' Kendrick smirked. 'Well these stamps. They have an amusing history. About two years ago one of the Russian top shots – no names, of course, dear Don – thought he was entitled to have his face on a postage stamp. Let's call him Mr J. Well, at that time Mr J was powerful enough to persuade the merry gang to agree and the order went ahead to print the stamps. Mr J had a jealous enemy who suddenly and unexpectedly produced proof that Mr J wasn't, after all, a loyal comrade but a thieving capitalist. The merry gang were horrified, stopped the print run of the stamps and ordered them all to be destroyed. It was inevitable, of course, that in the process Mr J also got himself destroyed. The merry gang realized that by stopping the print run of the stamps, the stamps already printed would be of tremendous value in the capitalist world. Fifteen thousand stamps had been printed. They were checked and eight were found to be missing. It was assumed that one of the printers had smuggled them out of the country for they turned up very briefly in Paris. A French stamp dealer approached a wealthy client of his, but before the client had time to make an offer, the French dealer was murdered and the stamps stolen. Since then, they have vanished but it is certain someone and not the Russians have them. A client of mine is ready to pay a substantial sum for them. For the past year he has made searching inquiries. Every big collector has been approached. They have, without exception, been frank about the approach, saying if they had the stamps they would accept the deal offered. My client is satisfied that they are being truthful. The one and only important philatelist who ignores my client is Larrimore. This seems to us to indicate that he has the stamps and won't part at any price, but we could be wrong. He just might be bloody minded. As you are a friend of his, we think it's possible for you to make certain he does have the stamps.'

'All this fuss about eight stamps?' Elliot said, staring at Kendrick. 'And all the same stamps? Just how much is your client willing to pay for them?'

Kendrick removed his wig, looked inside it as if he expected to find something growing in there and then replaced it.

'That we needn't go into, dear Don. All that is necessary for you to know is what we are going to pay you.'

'But why me? I'm an amateur. If your man is so keen to get the stamps why doesn't he hire experts to break into Larrimore's house and steal the stamps? Why me?'

Kendrick finished his whisky, blotted his mouth with a silk handkerchief and smiled.

'My dear boy! Larrimore owns around 300,000 stamps. How could a burglar find the wanted stamps among all those? What you need to find out is how he classifies his stamps. In what case he keeps his Russian stamps and how to get at them quickly. Without this knowledge, it would take weeks to find them.'

Elliot considered this.

'Yeah. Suppose I get near them? How do I know they're the stamps you want?'

'That is a good question.' Kendrick opened a drawer in his desk, took from it a steel box, found a key and opened the box. 'Here is a photostat of the stamp. It's nothing to look at and as you will see it is easily identified.' He passed the photostat across the desk.

Elliot examined the stamp. As Kendrick had said it was nothing to look at: the head of a man with the face of a charging bull and CCCP in the right hand corner.

'Well, okay ... I'll see what I can do,' Elliot said, putting the photostat back on the desk.

'You must be careful how you approach Larrimore,' Kendrick said quietly. 'He has already been offered a very large sum of money for the stamps and he has ignored the offer. If he has the stamps and if he becomes suspicious he might come under pressure, he could put the stamps in a bank vault. If he does that, then the operation will be sunk. So caution is the word.'

Elliot nodded.

'This is really a shot in the dark,' Kendrick went on. 'Although we feel it is highly likely that Larrimore has the stamps, we don't know for certain. As I have told you, my client has approached every likely collector and has drawn blank, but there might just possibly be some little collector and not Larrimore who has the stamps. So, first, you must find out if Larrimore has them. If he has them, you must find out where he keeps them.' Kendrick paused, then went on, 'I've been thinking, dear Don. It might be wiser if you got me this information – that he has the stamps and where he keeps them – and for me to pass this information on to my client for him to take action himself. We would still pay you the two hundred thousand and you would run no risk. What do you think?'

Elliot relaxed a little.

The thought of breaking into Larrimore's house, even with Vin to help him, had bothered him. If it was only information that Kendrick wanted, then the set-up looked much more reasonable.

'I'll go along with that. Okay, Claude, you leave this to me.'

Kendrick got to his feet. 'I have to run, cheri. A dreadful cocktail party looms ahead but it is good for business. One must sacrifice oneself. If there is anything further I can do to be helpful, do ask. I can rely on you to be most careful?'

'Sure ... I'm in this for the money... same as you.' Elliot got to his feet.

Kendrick waited until he heard Louis shut and lock the gallery door after Elliot, then he picked up the telephone receiver, dialled a number and waited. When the connection was made he said, 'The Belvedere Hotel? Please connect me with Mr Radnitz. This is Mr Claude Kendrick calling.'

*   *   *

Barney broke off to blot his eyes with the back of his wrist.

'These sausages, Mr Campbell, have a kick like a mule, but they are good for the digestion. You have one.'

I said a mule and my digestion were things apart and I would rather not.

Barney shrugged his immense shoulders, rinsed his mouth with some beer, collected his thoughts which apparently had been disturbed by the last sausage and settled down to his story again.

'Now, I bring upon the stage yet another character,' he said. 'Herman Radnitz.' He paused and blew out his cheeks.

'Radnitz comes to this City from time to time and rents all the year round the penthouse at this hotel, the Belvedere. Let me tell you the penthouse costs a lot of solid bread, but Radnitz is rich. I've seen him two or three times, and frankly, if I never saw him again, it wouldn't put me off my beer. Let me give you a photo of him. Imagine a short, square-shaped man with hooded eyes that would shame a bullfrog and a thick, hooked nose. I am told he is one of the richest men in the world and to my thinking looks the meanest sonofabitch I've yet seen and that, mister, is saying a lot.

'I'm told he is internationally known for his financial machinations, has power over foreign embassies, has fingers in any international deal worth more than five million dollars, is a power behind the Iron Curtain and is on first name terms with the political top shots throughout the world.

'This is the man who wanted Mr J's stamps. He has a vast organization of slaves who work for him and – so some people whisper – kill for him. He had instructed these people to find the stamps and after a year of systematic digging the gap had been narrowed to Larrimore.

'Radnitz found it an odd coincidence that the stamps just might be in his favourite City where he spent a few weeks a year relaxing. He had dealt with Kendrick's gallery and because he always believed in putting on file information about anyone he dealt with he had Kendrick investigated. He learned that Kendrick was not only a dealer in fine art, but also a fence. Having tried to approach Larrimore and failed, Radnitz decided to see what Kendrick could do.'

Barney paused to eat the last of the sausages. I waited until the expected reaction took place. Then when Barney had recovered, he said, 'You get the photo, Mr Campbell? Okay for me to go ahead or are there any questions?'

I said I was listening and there were no questions.

* * *

Ko-Yu, Radnitz's Japanese chauffeur and valet, opened the door of the luxury penthouse suite and bowed Kendrick inside.

'Mr Radnitz is expecting you, sir,' Ko-Yu said. 'Please to find him on the terrace.'

Kendrick went through the big living-room and out on to the terrace where Radnitz, wearing a short-sleeved shirt and cotton slacks was sitting at a table covered with documents.

'Ah, Kendrick, come and sit down,' Radnitz said. 'Would you like a drink?'

'No, thank you, sir,' Kendrick said and sat down away from the table.

Radnitz scared him, but he was sure this squat toad of a man could make money for him and money was the principal thing in Kendrick's life, apart, of course, from the glamour boys who buzzed around him like bees around a hive.

'Have you any news for me?' Radnitz asked, rolling a cigar between his stumpy fingers. 'The stamps?'

'There is progress, sir.' Kendrick explained about Elliot.

Radnitz listened, his eyes hooded.

'Larrimore has no friends,' Kendrick went on, 'except Elliot. I thought ...'

'Don't let's waste time,' Radnitz broke in curtly. 'I know all about Larrimore. Tell me about Elliot ... a movie star, if I remember rightly?'

Kendrick explained about Elliot's financial position: how he had lost his foot and how he, Kendrick, had put on the pressure and now how Elliot had agreed to co-operate.

'And you think he will succeed?'

'I hope so, sir.'

'And if he doesn't what other suggestions have you to make?'

Kendrick began to sweat. 'At the moment, I am relying on him, but if he fails, I will think of something.'

'And what does that mean?'

'Larrimore has a daughter,' Kendrick said. 'Perhaps we could use her to put pressure on Larrimore.'

'I am aware that he has a daughter,' Radnitz said stonily. 'Of course I have considered this possibility. But first we must be certain Larrimore has the stamps. If he has – if Elliot fails us – then we might use the daughter.'

'Yes,' Kendrick said, 'but I'm hoping Elliot won't fail … he has the incentive.'

'Very well. Keep me informed.' Radnitz made a gesture of dismissal. 'Thank you for coming,' and he reached for a document on the table.

When Kendrick had gone, Radnitz laid down the document and clapped his hands three times.

After a short delay his secretary and personal assistant came out on to the terrace. This man was tall, thin, balding, with deep set eyes and a thin, cruel mouth. His name was Gustav Holtz. He was as important to Radnitz as Radnitz's own right hand. A mathematical genius, a man with no scruples, with eight languages at his finger tips and with shrewd political know how, Holtz served Radnitz well.

'Don Elliot,' Radnitz said without looking around. 'One time movie star. Open a file on him. Have him covered. I want to be informed of his movements – a daily report. Be sure he doesn't become aware that he is being watched. Cover this immediately.'

'Yes, Mr Radnitz,' Holtz said.

Knowing his order would be scrupulously obeyed, Radnitz again picked up the document and dismissed Elliot from his mind.

* * *

As he drove back to the bungalow, Elliot did some heavy thinking. With Vin, Cindy and Joey willing to help him, he was now enthusiastic about getting hold of these Russian stamps. This seemed to him not only to be an exciting adventure and a solution to his financial problems but also a challenge in the best tradition of a movie plot. After Kendrick's warning, he realised a direct approach to Larrimore was out of the question. He hadn't seen Larrimore for more than three months. He had never been to his house. He couldn't 'accidentally' run into him at the golf club. He had to steer clear there. Too many of his creditors were members and besides, his subscription was long overdue. This wasn't going to be easy and his mind searched for another solution. Then he thought of Larrimore's daughter. She could be a possibility, he thought. Yes ... this could be the solution.

He was still thinking when he pulled up outside the bungalow.

He found Vin on his own. Joey and Cindy had just left in the Jaguar on a self service store raid.

After Elliot had explained the possibilities of stealing the stamps, Vin had become more co-operative. The thought of being paid fifty thousand dollars for stealing a few postage stamps appealed to him. In spite of the way Elliot had physically handled him, Vin was impressed by this handsome movie star. He felt instinctively that if anyone could plan this steal, Elliot would be the one to do it.

So when Elliot joined him in the back garden, Vin eyed him expectantly. He knew Elliot had been to talk to Kendrick and he was curious to know the outcome.

Elliot told him of the conversation.

'From what Kendrick tells me,' he concluded, 'it would be unwise to approach Larrimore. We have a problem here because I have to keep out of sight. By now, all my goddamn creditors will be looking for me. If they catch up with me, we're sunk. You've got to be the front man.'

'Suits me,' Vin said. 'So what do I do?'

'There's a good chance we can get the information we want from Larrimore's daughter. Judy Larrimore is a wild one. I've met her a number of times in various nightclubs. She's strictly not my style. She drinks too much, tries too hard and is my idea of a juvenile pest. Her father can't stand the sight of her – nor she him. Although she lives with him, they scarcely ever meet. He keeps her short of money so she is on the look out all the time for boyfriends who have money to spend on her. I'm sure you can handle her. I think she could have the information we want. Before Larrimore's wife died in an accident, he told me Judy helped him classify his stamps. It was only when she lost her mother that the girl went off the rails and has kept off them ever since. So she should know something about these Russian stamps, always providing Larrimore has them.'

Vin was listening with interest.

'Sounds right up my alley. So how do I meet this chick?'

'No trouble at all ... a straight pick up. One of her favourite haunts is the Adam and Eve club. She usually begins her night prowl there around ten o'clock. You can't miss her. She's around eighteen, tall, good figure and with red hair. She inherited her hair from her mother who was Italian. This Venetian red is unique ... you seldom see it here. If you spot a wild looking girl with red hair, wearing as little as she can, you can bet she's Judy Larrimore.'

'I like it even more,' Vin said with a leer. 'Sounds to me like fun and business combined.'

'Handle her carefully,' Elliot warned. 'She's no push over and she has the pick of the wild ones here, but she'll go for new blood if you approach her right. Don't rush her. We have time. After three or four meetings, you can begin to probe and I'll tell you how to handle it. Just get intimate now ... okay?'

Vin nodded. 'I'll get after her tonight.'

While they were talking, Joey and Cindy were working the local self service store. Cindy was busy filling her 'maternity basket' with items for the evening meal. She planned to make this a special dinner. Elliot had explained he couldn't return to his home and it would be risky for him to put up at a hotel, so how about moving in with them? Joey and Cindy welcomed this idea. Vin wasn't too happy about it, but when Elliot said he would pool his nine thousand dollars towards expenses and finance the steal he was quick to agree.

While Elliot had been explaining about the stamps, Vin, who missed little, had seen the way Cindy was looking at Elliot and he began to get the idea that Cindy was taking more interest in Elliot than was healthy. He had a sneaking feeling that because Elliot had manhandled him, Cindy was now transferring her affections from him to Elliot.

When Elliot had gone to see Kendrick and Joey and Cindy had gone to the self service store, Vin, alone, had time to think. Elliot was the key to the Big Take which he, Vin, was always dreaming about. He asked himself how much Cindy meant to him. He wasn't in love with Cindy – Vin just didn't know the meaning of love. He had thought it would be fun to be married to her, to take her around and to have a good time with her, but was there more in it than that? There were thousands of girls as pretty as Cindy: thousands as cute. If she wanted Elliot, he, Vin, would be nuts to spoil what looked like the Big Take. When they got the stamps and Elliot had paid over the fifty thousand dollars, if Cindy opted to stay with Elliot then that would be too bad for her and Joey. Vin grinned suddenly. He would pocket the whole amount and walk out on them. Elliot could take care of them. Why not? If she didn't go with Elliot, then fine, but he wasn't going to shed tears if she didn't.

Once having got this clear in his mind, he relaxed and was able to get along with Elliot.

Cindy had decided to cook a chicken casserole which she did very well. It took her a little time to find two chickens that satisfied her. While she was examining the birds, Joey regarded her with loving eyes. He had seen the change come over her since the clash between Elliot and Vin and in one way he was relieved, but in another way, worried. Vin at least was in Cindy's class, but Elliot wasn't. Elliot could just fool around with her and leave her flat and this had always been Joey's fear that Cindy could get hurt.

When the shopping was over and as they were walking to where Cindy had parked the Jaguar, Joey said, 'Elliot seems a nice fella, Cindy. What do you think?'

She nodded. As she got into the car, she said, 'Dad ... I've been thinking. I've made a mistake about Vin.'

Joey sighed. 'All women are allowed to make mistakes, baby,' he said. 'Is there someone else?'

'As if you didn't know.' Cindy gave him a crooked smile. 'Don ... the moment I met him...'

'Does he feel the same about you?'

'Of course not! I mean nothing to him.' She started the car and pulled out into the traffic. 'A cat can look at a king, but that's it, dad.' She pulled a little face. 'I want you to know I'm through with Vin. I'm going to tell him. We can work together, but now, I don't want to marry him.'

'No one ever said you had to,' Joey said. 'When this job's done, we'll go off together, Cindy. With our share of the money we can find a little place and take it easy for a while.'

Cindy nodded.

But there was an expression in her eyes that saddened Joey.

* * *

'You ever been to the Adam and Eve club?' Barney asked. He was staring gloomily at the empty plate that had contained the sausages. The regret on his fat face would have melted a heart of stone.

I said nightclubs weren't in my line and how about a few more sausages?

He brightened perceptively.

'Yeah ... that's what I call a constructive suggestion.' He signalled to Sam. 'The trouble with these sausages, Mr Campbell, is that they give a man a thirst.'

Sam brought over another plate of sausages and another beer.

'Nightclubs are special,' Barney said when Sam had returned to the bar. 'You either like them or you don't. The Adam and Eve club is strictly for the wild ones. From what I hear of the place a cultured gentleman like yourself wouldn't be found dead there.' He bit into a sausage, chewed, grunted, wiped his eyes and went on. 'Vin had no trouble in spotting Judy Larrimore. She was up at the bar with a couple of hippies and they were soaking up gin and water. The hippies were around her age with long matted hair and dirty beards. They had on matador trousers and frilled shirts and apart from their smell of dirt they looked like something that had stepped out of the ads from *Playboy*.

'Vin got close and ordered a whisky. It didn't take more than a few minutes for Judy to spot him. The two hippies were getting drunk and Vin could see she was bored with them. He saw her eyes light up as she looked him over. He thought she was the sexiest dish he had seen in years.

'He gave her his wide "come on" smile and she smiled back.

'One of the hippies – the bigger of the two – looked around and glared at Vin who met the glare with the grin he reserved for juveniles. The hippie then looked at Judy to see how she was reacting, but she was continuing to look Vin over.

'Vin thought it was the moment to start something, so he said, "If you're bored with these kids, baby, how about a drink with me?"

' "Piss off!" the hippie snarled, his eyes turning vicious.

' "Don't be rude, little punk," Vin said softly. "Or I'll have to spank you."

'Judy giggled and sliding around the hippies she joined Vin, moving slightly behind him.

'The other hippie threw the contents of his glass towards Vin's face, but that was old hat stuff to Vin. He moved aside and a girl coming up to the bar got splashed.

'Vin jabbed a left into the first hippie's face and the hippie's nose exploded into a red mush. When Vin hit, he hit. The other hippie tried to back away, but Vin reached him with a right hook that lifted him off his feet and slammed him flat on the floor.

'The girl who had got splashed was now screaming like a train whistle and the rest of the people in the bar were shouting. It all happened in seconds. Vin caught Judy by her arm and rushed her to the exit, and out into the hot night. She went willingly enough, stifling her laughter and they bundled into the Jaguar and Vin was driving away before the Club bouncer thought of moving into action.'

Barney paused to reach for another sausage.

'I won't waste time going into details, Mr Campbell. It's enough to say, Vin drove to a deserted part of the beach and he and Judy got out of the car and as soon as he had closed the car door he saw she had her pants off. He took her and she responded like she was demented. When it was over, she put her pants on and made for the car.

'Vin tried chatting her up, but she told him to shut his head and take her home. He thought his so called love making had rocked her so violently she wasn't in the mood to talk so he went along with her.

'He was pleased with himself. He imagined telling Elliot all the details of how he had got to first base after meeting Judy for only ten minutes. This achievement restored his confidence in himself. He would be able to prove to Elliot he was a better man than he, but he had an unpleasant surprise when he pulled up outside the gates leading to the Larrimore home.

' "Okay, baby," he said, getting out of the Jaguar. "How's about tomorrow night? Let's go and take the town apart."

"No ..." She got out of the car and started for the gates.

' "Hey! Wait a minute!"

'She paused and turned.

' "I said no."

' "What's the idea?" Vin demanded, puzzled, and he reached for her.

' "Keep your paws off me," she snapped. "We don't meet again ... you're not my thing," and she started again towards the gates.

'For a moment Vin stood rooted, not believing what he had heard, then he got a rush of blood to his head and he grabbed her arm and swung her around. He ran into a slap in the face that made his eyes blink and she wrenched free.

'Then out of the shadows came the two hippies. They had been waiting for the past hour. They had bicycle chains around their right fists and they came at Vin on either side of him.

' "Get him, boys!" Judy screamed. "Mark the bastard!"

'Vin had lived a life of violence. He couldn't remember how many times he had been in a spot like this and had survived. As Larry, the bigger of the hippies, slashed at his face with the chain, Vin ducked under the flaying steel, caught hold of Judy and flung her at Larry. They both went sprawling. The other hippie caught Vin across the neck with his chain. Weaving, Vin rushed him, grabbed his wrist, twisted him around and drove a crushing punch into the boy's kidneys. The hippie sank on to his knees, moaning.

'Larry was up and again his chain whistled towards Vin who just managed to duck under it, then Vin jumped forward and drove the top of his head into Larry's face. Larry's teeth gave as he was flung back. He tried to regain his balance, tripped over his own feet and fell. Stepping up to him, Vin kicked him in the side of his head and Larry went limp.

'Vin touched the side of his neck. Blood was dripping from the cut inflicted by the chain. He looked at the two hippies, satisfied he would have no more trouble from them, then he turned and looked at Judy.

' "How about tomorrow night, baby?" he asked quietly. "Suppose I pick you up here around nine?"

'Judy was staring at him, her eyes wide, then she suddenly laughed.

' "Man! That was something! Yes ... I'll be here."

'He went to her and pulled her to him. The blood from the cut on his neck dripped on to her bare shoulder.

' "Be here, baby," he said. "I wouldn't want to bust into your home and drag you out ... okay?"

' "Yes."

'He ran his hand over her body. She stood placid and let him. Then after squeezing her buttock, he shoved her away, strolled over to his car and drove off.

'On his return to the bungalow, he got Elliot aside and told him what had happened.

' "She's a little animal, but I've got her fixed," he said. "I know the type. The rougher you treat them, the harder they fall for you."

'But Elliot was worried. This seemed to him to be moving too fast.

' "Suppose she isn't there tomorrow night?"

'Vin grinned.

' "She'll be there. I've got what it takes, pally. I know how to handle women." '

* * *

She was there, standing outside the gates of the house when Vin drew up in the Jaguar at a minute after 21.00.

Vin grinned to himself as he leaned over to open the offside door. She had on a patterned Mexican shirt, hot pants and knee high boots. Her silky red hair fell in unruly waves to her shoulders and Vin again thought she was the sexiest dish he had seen in years.

'Hi, Superman!' she said as she got in and slammed the car door. 'See? Here I am.'

'Fine. You look good enough to eat,' Vin said, 'and talking about eating ... let's eat.'

With the car radio blaring swing, he drove fast to the Lobster and Crab restaurant at the far end of the waterfront. This was a small, expensive but 'with it' restaurant Elliot had told him about.

'It's just right for her,' Elliot said as he had given Vin three hundred dollars for spending money. 'Take it easy. Don't rush anything.'

Judy made an impact as she strutted into the restaurant. People stared at her and she enjoyed being stared at. Vin, following behind, realized that Elliot had made the right choice. This was away from the hippie scene and yet 'in' enough to appeal to Judy.

The Maitre d'hôtel, dressed as a pirate even to a black patch over his eye and skull and cross bones on his Napoleon hat, took them into an alcove to a table set for two away from the rest of the diners.

There was a Negro band playing violent jazz and the trumpeter was in the class of Louis Armstrong. You had to shout to each other to be heard.

Judy sat down and looked around, her eyes sparkling.

'Hey, Superman! This is my thing!'

'None of your kids bring you here?' Vin asked.

Her smokey green eyes hardened.

'Don't give me that. They're not such kids and I get along with them.'

'You're welcome.' Vin turned to the Maitre d'hôtel who had come up for their order. 'Let's have crab cocktails, steaks and all the trimmings and whisky sours.' Again Elliot had told him what to order.

'Yes, sir.' The Maitre d'hôtel went away.

'Don't ask me what I want to eat,' Judy said, glaring at him.

'Why should I? You're in the hamburger class, baby. You choose what you want when you're with the kids. I'll choose for you when you're with me.'

'Man! Don't you think you're perfect?'

'That's what I am.' He grinned at her. 'And you're not so lousy either.' He shoved back his chair. 'Let's dance.'

They danced and they ate and Vin could see Judy was enjoying herself. By the way she ate, he decided she was a strictly hamburger girl. As soon as they had finished, he paid the bill, letting her see the roll of five dollar bills he took carelessly from his pocket, then led her out into the hot night air.

'Come on, baby, let's kick this town apart,' he said, getting into the Jaguar.

'Where are we going now?'

'The Alligator Club,' Vin said. 'You know it?'

Judy's eyes popped wide open.

'Why, no ... that's strictly big time. Are you a member?'

'Why, sure. You mean none of your kids ever took you to the Alligator?' Vin asked. He had never been there himself but again Elliot had fixed things with a telephone call to the secretary of the club ... about the only club in the City where Elliot didn't owe money.

'Man!' Judy said under her breath. 'Let's go!'

They danced, drank and finally had a swim in the vast pool before leaving the club at 02.00.

'Now we get laid,' Vin said who was thoroughly enjoying himself. He found Judy an amusing companion. 'We'll go to the Blue Heaven motel. Okay?'

'Why not?'

During the evening he had told her he was an account executive, working for a top advertising agency in New York and was on vacation. Elliot had given him enough background details to make his cover stand up. Judy didn't seem interested in what he was but only became alert when he talked money. He could see that money was her only interest so he talked money.

'That's what I want,' Judy said, 'I want money. I want to get away from home, get away from my stinking father, live a life of my own.'

'What's the matter with your father?' Vin asked as he drove along the highway towards the motel.

'Matter? Don't talk wet! Every parent is a pain in the ass and anyway, my father's special. All he thinks about is postage stamps for God's sake!'

'What's so special about postage stamps?'

'Oh, the hell with it! Why talk about him?'

'Tell me ... I'm interested. Does he make money out of stamps?'

'He spends money, the old goat! He has thousands of goddamn stamps. You know something? He's been offered a million dollars for eight goddamn Russian stamps! A million dollars and the old ape wouldn't deal!'

Vin nearly drove off the highway. He swung the wheel wildly, got back on to the road as a driver of a car behind him honked on his horn.

'You drunk?' Judy demanded. The swerve at the speed they were driving at scared her.

'You never been drunk?' Vin said. 'Relax. I was listening to you and my mind strayed.'

'Man! Don't let it stray again.'

They drove in silence while Vin turned this sensational bit of information over in his mind.

These must be the stamps Elliot was after! he thought. Holy mackerel! Elliot was offering fifty thousand and here was this chick telling him they were worth a million!

A million!

He felt his mouth turn dry. Here was the Big Take! The real Big Take! His mind worked swiftly. If he handled this carefully and used his head there would be no need to split the take four ways. Elliot, Cindy and Joey could go to hell. After all he, Vin, was the front man. All he had to do was to get information from this stupid chick and he could cash in for a million! The thought brought him out into a sweat.

'What's the matter with you all of a sudden?' Judy asked crossly. 'Have you gone dumb on me?'

With an effort, he switched his attention back on her.

'You wait, baby,' he said, aware his voice sounded husky. 'Let's get to the motel ... I'll show you if I'm dumb or not.'

In another five minutes' driving, he turned off the highway and drove up a long twisty road that led to the motel.

He slid out, of the car, saying, 'I'll go fix it. You wait here.'

Minutes later he returned to the car, opened the offside door so Judy could get out and together they walked across to one of the cabins.

Elliot's warning not to rush things hammered in Vin's mind. They had the rest of the night. He must play this cool. A million dollars! Who could be the nut to offer all that bread for eight stamps? This, he told himself, he had to find out.

He unlocked the door of the cabin and they went in. The Blue Heaven motel, again recommended by Elliot, had deluxe cabins. A big room, furnished with modern lounging chairs, a settee, a colour TV set and a fully stocked bar, greeted them. There was a bedroom with a king size bed to their left and a bathroom to their right.

'Fancy,' Judy said approvingly as she looked around.

Vin shut and locked the door

The bed was prepared and inviting.

'Strip off, baby,' he said, 'and take a shower. I want to catch the late news.' He went over to the TV set and turned it on.

95

'What's so important about the news?' Judy asked as she slid out of her clothes.

'Never mind ... hurry it up,' Vin said curtly. He wanted her out of the way so he could think.

Now naked, Judy went into the bathroom and shut the door.

A million dollars! This was the only thought in Vin's head.

He stared at the lighted screen without registering what was going on while he thought. This chick wanted money. She had said so. If he handled her right, she and he could get the stamps and with her know how sell them for this lump of money. Maybe she could find out who had made the offer. She could for sure tell him how to get the stamps. A million! Sweet Judas! The thought made Vin's pulse rate bound.

Once he had the money he could deal with Judy. She wasn't his style. She was too tricky and tricky chicks weren't for him. Once they had the money, he would lose her.

But he must be careful, he warned himself. He mustn't rush it. So okay, he would play this cool. He turned off the TV as Judy came out of the bathroom.

He got to his feet and grinned at her.

'Come and get it,' she said and going to the bed, she lay down, swung up her long legs and beckoned to him.

5

It was while they were eating breakfast on the patio, the morning sun shining on them, that Vin began his probe.

'If I'm going to make it a regular thing to go around with you, Superman,' Judy was saying, 'I'm going to get fat.'

She was engaged in eating a breakfast of grapefruit, eggs and grilled ham, toast and coffee, and she was eating as if she hadn't had a meal in days.

Vin had settled for orange juice, coffee and a cigarette. He grinned.

'This is what comes of going around with kids, baby,' he said. 'They can't afford to feed a girl like you. Don't worry about getting fat. I'll give you enough exercise to keep your weight down.'

Judy giggled.

'You've got something ... hang on to it.'

'Tell me about your old man,' Vin said casually. 'You two don't get along together?'

'That's the understatement of the year,' Judy said, buttering toast. 'I don't want to talk about him. He gives me a pain in my ass.'

'But these stamps you were telling me about.' Vin reached for another cigarette. 'You said someone offered him a million for eight stamps. Were you putting me on?'

'No. I saw the letter on his desk.' She heaped marmalade on the toast. 'You could have knocked me down with a whisky bottle.'

'You mean some crackpot actually offered your old man all that bread for eight goddamn stamps?'

'That's it. It made me sick to my stomach. All that money! What I could do with it! The stupid old bastard just threw the letter in the trash basket.'

'Just what are these stamps?'

She shrugged. 'Oh, something he got hold of. People are always sending him stamps. I don't know. Look, Superman, let's skip my old man. Let's talk about something else.'

Vin poured himself another cup of coffee.

'Who is this guy who offered all this money?'

Judy paused as she began to butter another piece of toast. Her green eyes suddenly became quizzing.

'Why should you care?'

Vin realized he was out on thin ice.

'So you don't know?'

'Suppose I do?'

'Well, okay, baby, if you want to make a mystery of it.' He shrugged. 'I was just curious.'

'Oh, let's skip stamps.' She munched the toast. 'Let's go swimming. I know a marvellous place where you can swim in your skin.'

'Fine.' Remembering Elliot's advice not to rush it, Vin reluctantly decided to drop his probe for the time being.

After they had finished breakfast and Vin had paid the check for the night's stay, they went together to the Jaguar.

They drove some twenty miles along the coast road and then down a narrow sandy lane that led to a small deserted cove with access to the sea.

They left the car, stripped off and swam, then getting under the shade from a clump of palms, they stretched out, side by side.

'This is the life,' Judy said. 'Man! If I could do this every day! Are you staying long, Superman?'

'What would you do if you had a million dollars, chick?' Vin asked, staring up at the overhanging palm leaves.

'Still got that on your mind?' Judy turned on her side and studied him. 'What's with it?'

'I'm asking you a question,' Vin said, not looking at her.

'So okay ... with that kind of bread I'd get out of this goddamn country. I'd go to Paris and buy myself a ritzy apartment and get into the life there ... the life I want to live. I'd have a ball. I'd have another place in Capri. I'd have a ball there too. With all that money, the men would come. I wouldn't even have to look for them.'

'If your old man has all these stamps would he miss these eight if you took them?' Vin asked.

Judy remained silent for so long, Vin got worried that he had rushed this too fast, then she said, 'Yes, he'd miss them. He spends most of his time gloating over his stamps and now this guy has offered all this money, I bet he gloats over those stamps more than the others.'

'What guy?'

Judy sat up, cupping her naked breasts. 'You may think I'm dim, Superman, but I'm going to surprise you. Are you thinking of trying to get these stamps and selling them to this man who has made this offer?'

This was it, Vin thought. He had rushed it, but this could be his chance. He turned on his side and looked up at her.

'It's an idea that occurred to me,' he said. 'It we get a pay off like that we would split it down the middle or, if you want to stick with me, we could share the lot and have a real ball together.'

They stared at each other.

'Just who are you?' she asked. 'That account executive crap doesn't jell with me. Who are you?'

'A guy on the make.' Vin grinned. 'Like you: thirsty for money. You and me could work this ... as partners.'

She got to her feet and with a towel she wiped the sand off her buttocks and thighs. He lay there, watching her, tense, wondering if he had played the wrong card or the right card too fast. He felt a growing uneasiness as she dressed in silence.

'Well, for Pete's sake! Say something!'

She looked down at him. 'Let me tell you something, Superman. I don't trust anyone and that includes you. If you think you're smart enough to get those stamps I'll help you, but you don't get the name of the man who wants to buy them. I'll handle that end of it. And if there is going to be a split, it'll be a split on my terms. Seven fifty for me and two fifty for you.'

A tricky chick, Vin thought. Okay, let's play along. Get the stamps, then I'll take over. If she imagines she's going to have that kind of split then she needs her head examined, but okay, let's play along.

He got up and put on his clothes while she wandered over to the Jaguar. When he had dressed, he joined her.

'Let's have a drink,' she said, getting into the car. 'I'm as thirsty as a camel.'

He took her to a beach bar and bought her a double gin and tonic while he had a beer. It was still too early for the bar to be crowded so they sat at an isolated table under the awning and Vin began to work on her.

'How do we get the stamps, baby?' he asked.

She regarded him.

'You're keen, aren't you?'

'Skip the smart dialogue,' Vin said sharply. 'Are we going to work together on this or aren't we?'

She sipped her drink while she continued to eye him.

'Do you imagine, Superman, that if there was a chance, I wouldn't have taken the stamps weeks ago, sold them and got the hell out of here? It's no deal. The old stinker has his collection protected.'

'Maybe with the two of us working at it, we could swing it.'

She shook her head. 'This is a waste of time. You won't get them so forget it. Let's talk about what we're going to do tonight.'

'Where money is concerned,' Vin said, 'nothing is a waste of time. Where does he keep his collection?'

'In the house. He has a big room, lined with drawers. In each drawer there are stamps set out under glass and each drawer is wired to a burglar alarm. There are hundreds of drawers and thousands of stamps. Believe me, looking for one particular stamp is like looking for a virgin in this City ... strictly for the birds.'

'What's his security like?'

'Tricky alarms wired direct to the cop house. Each drawer automatically locks when he throws a switch when he isn't in the stamp room. The switch is in a steel box built into the wall and he always has the key. There is a closed circuit TV and the monitor is watched by Security Guards, night and day when he isn't in the room.' She grimaced. 'He takes care of his stamps ... that's all he cares about.'

Vin turned this information over in his mind. After a long pause, he said, 'Okay ... but suppose I got in the stamp room without raising the alarm, how do I find these eight stamps?'

101

She stared at him, then laughed. 'You don't get in.'

'I said suppose I did.'

She shrugged. 'You'll find something like eight hundred drawers all containing thousands of stamps, all under glass and the drawers wired to the cop house and watched by Security Guards so if you touch just one of the drawers you'll get a lapful of fuzz.'

Burglar alarms, closed circuit TV and police didn't bother Vin. He was an expert in his field, but what did bother him was the thought of getting into this stamp room and then trying to find eight particular stamps.

'Look, baby,' he said, 'your old man can't have a miracle memory. Suppose he wants one particular stamp among all these thousands? He must have a system of finding it fast.'

'He has. He and I worked it out together ... that was before mummy died and before I realized there was more to life than fooling around with a lot of crappy stamps.'

Vin felt his pulse rate quicken.

'What's the system then?'

'It's simple. Each drawer has a number. He keeps a register. For instance USA stamps are in drawers numbered one to a hundred and fifty. These drawers are broken down into dates and again into rare stamps. During the day he carries the register around with him and at night he locks it in a safe in his bedroom.'

'What's it look like?'

'A little leather loose leaf book he carries in the inside pocket of his jacket. Short of knocking the old buzzard on the head, no one will get it.'

Vin finished his drink.

'So suppose we knock him on the head?'

'Not a chance. He only goes out once a week to play golf, otherwise he's in the stamp room. When he goes to the golf club he has a chauffeur with him. The road to the club is always busy with traffic so no one can hold up the car. There's no chance of getting into the house. He has a staff of five and they're always around. You can forget it. Without the register, you can forget the stamps ... so you can forget the million dollars.'

Vin now had most of the information he wanted. There was no point in wasting further time with this chick.

'Okay ... I'll think about it. If I come up with an idea, do you and me make a deal?'

'What deal?'

'I get the stamps. You give me the name of the buyer and we split the take.'

'That's not my idea of a deal, Superman,' she said and finished her drink. 'I take seven fifty and you have the rest.'

Vin grinned. 'Okay ... okay.'

'And I handle the buyer, Superman.'

Just for a moment he hesitated, then, knowing she had him where she wanted him for the moment, he grinned again.

'It's a deal.'

She nodded.

'Well, let's go.' He got to his feet. 'I've got business. How about tomorrow night?'

'What's the matter with tonight?'

He shook his head. 'I'm tied up. Tomorrow night I'll take you to the Low Life Club. Dress the part baby ... it's your thing.'

'Who's tying you up tonight?' She was studying him suspiciously.

'Oh, a guy... come on, baby, let's go.'

She went with him to the Jaguar.

'Want me to drop you off home?' he asked as he started the car.

'Who wants to go home? Drop me off at the Plaza Beach. I'll spend the day there.' As he set the car in motion, she went on, 'Give me some money, Superman. If I'm not seeing you tonight, I've got to eat. Give me a hundred dollars.'

'Your kid friends can feed you. I only give money for value.'

'Haven't you had value, you mean sonofabitch?' she demanded.

'Not yet.' Vin grinned. 'You, me and a million bucks is my idea of value.' But when he dropped her at the entrance to the Plaza Beach he gave her thirty dollars.

She snatched the money out of his hand, put her tongue out at him, then walked away, swinging her hips.

*   *   *

For the first time since he had become secretary to Herman Radnitz, Holtz failed to carry out his master's instructions.

He had been told to have Don Elliot watched and to submit a daily report on Elliot's activities. Back in his office, he had telephoned Jack Lessing who was in charge of a team of experts specializing in this kind of work. Lessing had said there would be no problem and he would put four men on the job right away.

Six hours later, Lessing, short, thin, with foxy eyes and thinning hair, came into Holtz's office. Without wasting time, he reported that Elliot had disappeared and his men could find no trace of him.

'I've got ten men hunting for him but up to now there's no sign of him,' Lessing said. 'He hasn't left the City by rail or plane but he could have used his car. His Alfa is missing. We can't get a thing from his servants. So what do you want me to do?'

Holtz stared at him and the expression in his eyes made Lessing shift uneasily.

'Find him!' Holtz snarled. 'That's your job ... that's what you get paid for! It can't be difficult. He's known everywhere. Get the syndicate working on it ... get every available man on it but find him!'

When Lessing had left, Holtz sat wondering if he should wait another six hours before telling Radnitz. There was every chance that with the whole of Lessing's organization hunting for Elliot he would be found, but he decided he would have to tell Radnitz there was a hitch.

He went out on to the terrace where Radnitz was talking to Berlin on the telephone. He was arranging a currency deal and Holtz waited until he had replaced the receiver.

'What is it?' Radnitz asked, turning to stare at Holtz.

Holtz told him and went on to explain what action was being taken. Radnitz listened, his fat face darkening and his hooded eyes gleaming angrily.

Holtz expected to receive vitriolic criticism. He was even prepared to be dismissed and he was startled when Radnitz seemed to control his anger and pointing to a chair, said quietly, 'Sit down.'

A little uneasy because he had never sat down in Radnitz presence before, Holtz took the chair.

'How long have you worked for me?' Radnitz asked, taking a cigar from a pigskin case and cutting it with a gold cutter.

'It will be five years next month, sir.'

Radnitz nodded. 'You have given satisfaction. You have my confidence. I think I had better tell you why Elliot must be found.'

Holtz stiffened. This was the last thing he expected and because he was surprised, he decided to say nothing.

Radnitz lit his cigar, then stared at the distant beach, crowded with people sun bathing and swimming.

'I am searching for eight Russian stamps,' he said. 'They come from a lot that was never issued to the public. They got into the hands of a Russian scientist who had fallen in love with an American woman he had met in East Berlin. He was warned to have nothing further to do with her. Outwardly he agreed, but inwardly he planned to defect. He knew the stamps would be valuable and he had to provide for himself and this woman once he left Russia. He drew up a report of his work. This report is of considerable value to the enemies of Russia. He made eight microdots of his report and each dot went on to each of the eight stamps, making them priceless. We needn't go into the details about the report but it is something the CIA would pay enormous money to have. This scientist persuaded a friend to smuggle the stamps out of Russia and to East Berlin and the American woman got them but the scientist had left it too late and he was arrested. Under torture he revealed what he had done. Having been warned of her lover's arrest, the woman fled to Paris. She sold the stamps to a Paris dealer and with the proceeds went to New York. The dealer, knowing nothing about the microdots, sold the stamps to a client who was kidnapped, but died of a heart attack before the kidnappers could find out what he had done with the stamps. The stamps have vanished.' Radnitz paused while he tapped ash off his cigar, 'As you know I have considerable and profitable dealings with the Soviet Government. They asked me if I could help. I have promised to do so. Financed by them, I have made a very thorough search for the missing stamps. Unfortunately, the news has been leaked to the CIA and they too are searching for the stamps. I have to move carefully. At the moment the CIA are concentrating their search among the smaller collectors – especially the Russian collectors. My search has narrowed down to a man called Paul Larrimore who lives in this City. I believe he has them and I have made him a generous offer which he has ignored. This means nothing. He either has the stamps and won't sell or he hasn't got them and hasn't the politeness to say so. It would be a simple solution to kidnap this man and force him to admit he either has or hasn't got the stamps, but this would produce publicity and would alert the CIA.' Radnitz puffed smoke, his face stony. 'I have now approached Claude Kendrick who knows this movie star, Elliot, who seems to be Larrimore's only contact. Elliot is desperate for money and has agreed to try to get information about the stamps. I have reason not to trust Kendrick. If Elliot got the stamps and gave them to Kendrick, Kendrick might try to find a higher bidder than myself so it is important for me to know when Elliot gets information and when he gets the stamps. So Elliot must be found at once.'

Holtz thought for a moment.

'If he is going to try for the stamps, sir, he will still be in the city. This narrows the field. I will alert Lessing.'

'I will leave it to you.' Radnitz paused and stared at Holtz. 'I've explained this to you because I want you to realize how important and how serious this operation is. If I get the stamps I will be in an excellent position to bargain with the Russians. The Kazan dam project is hanging fire. If I give them the stamps, they will give me the contract for the dam. It's as simple as that. I don't have to tell you how valuable the contract is. I expect to hear Elliot has been traced within the next twenty-four hours.' By way of dismissal, Radnitz reached for the telephone receiver.

*　　*　　*

A lot of questions ran through Vin's mind as he drove back to the bungalow.

Did Elliot know the real value of the stamps? Did Kendrick know? Just how much had Kendrick offered Elliot – a lot more than the fifty thousand Elliot was offering him, Cindy and Joey, that was for sure – but how much more?

Then he thought over the information he had got from Judy. The actual steal didn't worry him. He was sure he could handle the alarms and the closed circuit TV but how to get hold of the register? Various ideas occurred to him, but each was dismissed as too dangerous. He decided he would have to consult Elliot. Vin knew his own abilities were not up to organizing a tricky steal like this. One slip, one false move and a million dollars would escape him. The thought made him sweat. No, he would have to give Elliot some of Judy's information. Then if they were successful and got the stamps, he would have to fix Elliot and also Judy. He had already made up his mind there was going to be no share out on this steal. It was going to be the Big Take for him and nothing for the rest of them.

He found Elliot, Cindy and Joey in the garden. They looked expectantly at him as he came over and took the fourth chair.

'Where have you been?' Joey asked. 'We were getting worried. What's been going on?'

'Plenty.' Vin grinned. 'I've got this Larrimore babe eating out of my hand and I've got most of the info we want.'

'That's quick.' Elliot looked startled. 'You mean you've already talked to her about the stamps?'

'Sure ... it was a natural. She brought the stamps up herself.'

'Has Larrimore got them?'

Vin pointed his finger at Elliot. 'Just hold it, buster ... I'll ask the questions. How much did Kendrick offer you for these stamps?'

'It's not what he offered me that concerns you,' Elliot said quietly. 'You three agreed to work with me for fifty thousand dollars.'

Vin shook his head. 'Not now, buster. I'm doing all the work. You couldn't get to first base without me. These stamps are worth money ... so let's hear what Kendrick offered you.'

Elliot hesitated, then shrugged. 'Two hundred thousand. As it is my idea and my contact, fifty thousand is a fair spilt for you three.'

'You think so?' Vin was very sure of himself. 'I say no. It's going to be better than that.'

Elliot looked at Cindy and Joey.

'Are you satisfied with the split ... do you want more?'

'Never mind about them. I want more.' Vin said, 'and I'm going to get it. Here's the new deal. I get fifty, they get fifty between them and you get a hundred.'

Listening, knowing that once the operation was concluded, he and Cindy would be rid of Vin, Joey said quietly, 'That still puts you ahead, Mr Elliot.'

Elliot thought for a moment. This cut in the take would mean a few months less to live and he realized he was now ceasing to care.

'Okay, you have yourself a deal. Has he the stamps?'

'Yes.' Vin went on to explain about the register. 'This is the problem. Without this index, we'll never find the stamps. But once we know the number of the drawer containing the stamps I can get them.'

'This isn't our problem.' Elliot said. 'The deal I made with Kendrick is that if I can assure him Larrimore has the stamps and tell him how to find them, he'll pay off. You've given me the necessary information. We don't have to do anything more. It's his problem to get the stamps. By this time tomorrow we will have the money and can get out of town.'

Vin squinted at him.

'If a slob like Kendrick is willing to pay two hundred grand to you, how much do you imagine he is going to get when he sells the stamps?'

'That's his affair,' Elliot said impatiently. 'A hundred thousand is enough for me. I'll see him right away, give him this information and arrange for payment.'

'Hold it! Suppose I tell you I can find out who the buyer Kendrick is dealing with? Suppose I tell you this buyer would pay five hundred big ones and this could come to us instead of Kendrick?'

Elliot stared at him.

'Do you know who the buyer is?'

'I can find out.'

'How?'

Vin grinned. 'Don't worry about that. I'm not kidding. I can find that out. Now listen, we would be nuts to deal direct with Kendrick. That slob will pay you two hundred and put three hundred in his pocket for nothing. With my info we can get the stamps and then we can sell them to Kendrick's man for five hundred grand, cutting Kendrick out of the deal.'

Looking at Vin's excited face and seeing the greed in his eyes, Elliot suddenly felt sure that Vin was planning to double cross not only Kendrick but Cindy, Joey and himself. Just how the double cross would work Elliot had no idea, but he was sure this was what Vin was planning.

He felt a surge of excitement run through him. This could be much more fun than living in debt and pitying himself because he had a tin foot. He had made six successful movies in which he, as the hero, had pitted his wits against thugs like Vin. The scriptwriters had taken care that his wits had always been sharper and that always in the end he had come out top. But now, this was for real: not a thriller that was put in a can and exhibited in the movie houses of the world. There would be no scriptwriter to take care of him. No director to shout 'Cut!' when the going got too rough.

Okay, he thought, let's see how smart you are. Let's act this out as if it were a movie. What have I got to lose anyway? A few more months of life? If I don't get the money, there are the sleeping pills to take care of the final fade out. So I'll pretend to play along with you. Could be I'll be trickier than you think you are. At least, it could be fun ... acting out one of my movies, but this time for real.

'It's an idea,' he said. 'So what do you plan to do?'

Vin moved uneasily.

'Let's take another look at this: we have now the chance of getting five hundred grand. Let's work out a new deal. Joey and Cindy get a hundred and you and me get two hundred each. How about it?'

Joey was listening and worrying. A hundred thousand dollars! This was money beyond his dreams. He cringed at the thought of the prison sentence Cindy and he could get if this operation turned sour.

'No ... count us out!' he exclaimed. 'We've never done a job this big and we don't want to do it now!'

Vin looked contemptuously at the old man.

'Okay, then pull out. Elliot and I can swing it without either you or Cindy. So, okay ... go back to your small time if that's the way you want it.'

Cindy leaned forward, her eyes sparkling.

111

'It's not the way I want it!' she said. 'I'm sick of small time.' She looked at Joey. 'Okay, dad, if you want to pull out I won't try to persuade you but I'm staying in!'

Joey stared helplessly at her, then he lifted his hands in despair.

'Now, listen, baby ...'

'I'm staying in! That's final!'

Joey looked at Elliot.

'Well, Mr Elliot, so we stay in, but how can we help? I don't see how we come into this.'

'That's where the wonder boy earns his cut,' Vin said. 'I can fix the alarms and get the stamps if I know where they are. That's my job and I can do it. Elliot has to dream up an idea of getting the register from Larrimore. If he can't use you two, you're out anyway. This take is strictly for workers.'

Cindy looked hopefully at Elliot.

'We know Larrimore carries the register around in his inside jacket pocket,' Elliot said after a moment's thought. 'At night the register is locked in a safe in his bedroom.' He looked at Vin. 'Right?'

'Yeah.'

'Joey ... do you think you could steal the register off Larrimore if you got close to him?'

Joey didn't hesitate. 'Yes ... that's no problem.'

'Suppose we have a demonstration.' Elliot got to his feet and went into the bungalow. From the bookcase he took a paperback and put it in his inside jacket pocket, then he came back into the garden.

'I have a book in my jacket pocket, Joey. Let's see you get it.'

Cindy was on her feet and moving by Elliot she appeared to stumble and lurched against him.

'Sorry,' she said. 'My foot slipped. Go on, dad, show him.'

Joey grinned uneasily. 'It's gone, hasn't it, Mr Elliot?'

Cindy was holding the paperback in her hand.

'Impressive,' Elliot said. 'Okay, I'll think about it.'

Leaving them, he went to his bedroom and lay on the bed. He lay thinking, staring up at the ceiling for the next hour. Then when Cindy called that lunch was ready, he got up and joined the other three in the small dining-room.

'Got an idea, buster?' Vin asked as he cut into the steak on his plate.

'The problem is to get to Larrimore,' Elliot said. 'He only goes out in his car. He doesn't receive visitors, but I have an idea that might work.' He looked at Cindy. 'You would have to handle it. After seeing your demonstration I think you could do it. Here's the idea: Larrimore gets a letter telling him the undersigned – that's you, Cindy – has inherited a collection of stamps left to you by your grandfather. You have heard dealers offer little or nothing for valuable stamps. You have no idea if the collection is valuable or not. You are asking him, as you have heard he is a famous philatelist, if he would look at the stamps and if there are any of interest to advise you. I think that is the kind of bait Larrimore might rise to. You'll say your grandfather started the collection when he was young. That might make Larrimore think there could be a few valuable stamps in the album. He might invite you to call on him. If he does, then it is up to you to get the register off him. We know the stamps are indexed under countries. If you get hold of the register and while he is examining your stamps, find the CCCP section, you could be lucky to find the number of the drawer which contains the eight stamps we want. This is a long shot but it might come off. What do you think?'

113

'That's bright,' Vin said, annoyed he hadn't thought of this himself. 'It could work.'

'I'll do it,' Joey said. 'I don't want Cindy to do it.'

Elliot shook his head.

'I'm sorry, Joey, but Cindy must do it. With her looks, she would throw Larrimore off his guard. A young girl coming to him for advice will flatter him.' He looked at Cindy. 'Shall we try?'

Cindy nodded.

'Okay. I'll draft a letter for you to write.' Elliot looked over at Joey. 'Will you go down to the waterfront and take a look at the junk shops there? I'm sure you'll find an old stamp album full of trash that you can pick up for a few dollars. The older it looks the better. Then go to one of the better stamp dealers and buy three or four good stamps. They must be around 1900, not more recent. Tell the dealer you want to give them as a gift and you know nothing about stamps. Pay up to four hundred dollars. We've got to make this album a little interesting or Larrimore might get suspicious.'

Joey nodded.

Elliot finished his steak and pushed his plate away.

'Now you, Vin ... how are you finding out who the buyer is?'

Vin's eyes shifted. 'You can leave that to me. I'll find out.'

'That's not good enough. We're working together as a team. We want to know. How are you finding out?'

Vin thought quickly. He realized that without Cindy, he wouldn't get the register. He had to be careful not to alert Elliot's suspicions that he planned a double cross.

'Judy Larrimore knows who he is.'

Elliot cut himself a slice of cheese, then pushed the cheese plate over to Vin. 'How did she find out?'

114

'She read a letter she found on her old man's desk.'

'Why hasn't she told you who the buyer is?'

Vin felt a trickle of sweat run down his face.

'She'll tell me. I've got to soften her up a little.'

'And how do you do that, Vin?'

Elliot's probing eyes made Vin look away.

'I'll fix it ... leave it to me.'

'Sorry, Vin, you're not convincing,' Elliot said. 'Let's get this straight. We've just made a deal ... remember? We four are now partners. You're holding something back. I want to know what it is. I want to know more about this babe who, you tell me, eats out of your hand.'

Vin shifted in his chair.

'She wants money, but I'll pay her off ... I'll do that out of my share. For a grand she'll give me the name of the buyer. That's all there's to it.'

'Then why didn't you say so before?'

'It's a deal I did with her. Why should I bother you with that for God's sake?'

'So you've told her you are planning to steal the stamps?'

Vin took out his handkerchief and wiped his face. He saw Joey and Cindy were staring at him and there was suspicion in their eyes.

'So what? Look ... this babe hates her old man. She couldn't care less what happens to his stamps.'

'But she knows you are planning to steal the stamps?'

'What if she does?'

'You ask yourself that one, Vin.' Elliot got to his feet. 'I'll get that letter drafted, Cindy.' Turning to Joey, he went on, 'Will you take care of the stamp album?'

The three left the room.

Vin hacked a slice of bread from the loaf and cut himself another piece of cheese.

'I'll have to watch this sonofabitch,' he told himself. 'He's going to be tricky.'

        *   *   *

Jack Lessing returned to his office. Holtz had given him an ultimatum: find Elliot or lose the Radnitz account and since the account was worth many thousands a year to Lessing and since his ten men had still found no trace of Elliot, he was more than worried.

'Try everything,' Holtz had said. 'He's got to be found and found fast! We know he is in the City. We know he might try to contact Paul Larrimore, the philatelist. As he owes money everywhere you won't find him in his usual haunts. He must have holed up somewhere. Check every small hotel, even the rooming houses. Look out for his Alfa: you've got the licence number. He's got to be found.'

Lessing put another twenty men, drawn in from Miami and Jacksonville with instructions to check the hotels and fast, then he sent for Harry Orson and Fay Macklin, two of his top investigators. He told them the problem.

Orson, a powerfully built man in his late thirties, was noted for his patience and bulldog determination. Nondescript to look at, shrewd and an easy mixer, he was the ideal man hunter.

Fay Mackiln, mousey looking, small, around thirty-five years of age, had a talent for being in a place and never being noticed.

'Elliot is thought to be trying to contact Paul Larrimore ... just why, Holtz didn't say,' Lessing said. He pushed a folder across his desk. 'That will give you all the dope about Larrimore. He seems our best bet. Quite close to his house is an empty villa. I've fixed it for you two to get in there and watch his place. I want the dope on everyone who visits Larrimore. Elliot, being a movie star, may try to play it smart. He might arrive in disguise. So check out everyone who calls on Larrimore. You will have two operators to help you. I want you to watch and alert them when someone calls.'

An hour later, Orson and Macklin were installed in an empty upper room of the villa which offered an uninterrupted view of the gates, the garden and the front door of Larrimore's house. They settled down to an alternate watch, equipped with powerful field glasses, a transceiver, camp stools and a hamper of food. Their wait was long and uneventful, but they were used to long, uneventful waits and that was why Lessing had picked them to watch Larrimore's house. At the end of the road, in a parking lot, two investigators in their cars sat waiting. Twice during the long day they were alerted to check trunks that had arrived at Larrimore's house but the report was negative: just a delivery of food. Then around midday, Orson saw Judy come out of the house, get into her beat up Austin Cooper and drive down to the gates. He immediately alerted one of the waiting investigators who caught up with Judy as she waited for a change of traffic lights.

'The girl's Larrimore's daughter,' Orson told the investigator over the transceiver. 'Stick with her, Fred. I'll get Alec to replace you later.'

'Okay and out,' Fred Nisson, said.

Half an hour later, Nisson radioed in that Judy was at the Plaza Beach surrounded by long haired freaks. What was he to do?

'Stick with her,' Orson said. 'Keep reporting in.'

At 15.00 Orson called Lessing. So far the operation was negative. No sign of Elliot. Every caller – and there had only been three of them – had been checked out. Nisson was watching the daughter who seemed settled to spend the day at the Plaza Beach.

Lessing cursed, told Orson he would send a relief for Nisson and then reported to Holtz.

* * *

Barney paused here to marshal his thoughts. He reached for the last sausage on the plate, regarded it thoughtfully before conveying it to his mouth.

'These sausages are enough to wake up a dead man,' he said. 'You don't know what you're missing.'

I said I believed in letting the dead lie in peace.

'Yeah.' Barney took a swig of beer, pushed away the empty plate, heaved a sigh and settled to talk again.

'Joey picked up a battered looking stamp album full of junk but he got four good stamps from a dealer that cost four hundred dollars. These Elliot put in the album.

'Elliot got Cindy to rewrite the letter to Larrimore he had drafted and that was sent off. There was nothing else for them to do but wait.

'But Vin had things to do. He had a date with Judy the following evening. He had a lot of thinking to do and as thinking wasn't his strong point, he worried.

'Until he was sure that Cindy's part of the operation succeeded, he couldn't make plans. But if Cindy did manage to find out in which drawer the stamps were then he would have to think fast and thinking fast always bothered Vin.

'He had a suspicion that Elliot was on to him. He also had a suspicion that unless he watched Judy closely, she could double cross him. Vin wasn't geared for this kind of set up and he knew it, but he was determined to get his hands on a million dollars.

'Elliot told them they couldn't expect an answer – if they were going to get an answer – from Larrimore for at least a week. They must try to relax and be patient.

'This was something Vin couldn't do in his present mood and he drove off in the Jaguar to explore the country, look in at a bar or two and take a swim.

'Cindy and he had had a talk. This was something he was expecting. Her no wedding bells and I'm sorry Vin line left him cold. He grinned at her and shrugged. "Okay, baby, if that's the way you want it," he said. "Maybe you're right. You stick to your old man. That way you won't get pregnant." That was the way Vin talked: no consideration for women.' Barney grimaced. 'I always say a woman should be shown consideration, Mr Campbell ... right?'

I said it was an accepted thing but there were women and women.

Barney let that one go with the breeze.

'So in the evening, Cindy found herself alone with Elliot. Joey was a TV addict and he was indoors, glued to the goggle box. Cindy and Elliot were sitting in the back garden with a big yellow moon looking down on them, the smell of jasmine in the air and the distant sound of an owl to make the set up pretty romantic.

'Elliot had discovered something about Cindy he hadn't found in any of the girls he had previously known. There was a restfulness about her that made her company easy. He felt he didn't have to keep talking to keep her interest. She didn't have to keep talking to keep his interest: just to sit with her in silence pleased him. This hadn't happened to him before.

' "Cindy ... about Vin," he said suddenly. "You told me you two were planning to get married."

' "Yes." Cindy looked up at the moon. "But not now. I've changed my mind. I've told Vin ... I think he's glad."

' "And you?"

' "Yes, I'm glad." She shrugged. "He seemed so glamorous and so confident ... I had never met anyone quite like him. But now ..."

' "Do you trust him, Cindy?"

'She stiffened and looked quickly at him.

' "What do you mean?"

' "You see, Cindy, all this is something new to me ... this four handed partnership. I feel I can trust your father and you, but not Vin. I may be wrong, but that's the way I feel right now."

' "Dad and I have talked about it ... yes, we feel like you ... we don't trust him, but without him we can't work this, can we?"

' "Without us, he can't work it either."

'Cindy nodded.

' "Dad said for me not to worry ... he said you would take care of Vin."

' "That's touching." Elliot reached out and took her hand. "Well, we'll see. This money means a lot to you two, doesn't it?"

'Cindy's heart was now beating so fast she could scarcely breathe. The casual touch of Elliot's hand turned her mind upside down.

' "I don't know ... Dad will arrange something." She pulled free and got to her feet. "I'd better see what he is doing ... he doesn't like being left alone for long."

' "Cindy!"

'She paused, looking down at him, her face flushed. He smiled up at her.

' "Let's forget him ... let's forget everything ... let's go for a swim." He looked intently at her. "I want to show you my tin foot." '

6

At 21.00 Orson got his first encouraging lead. He was at the window overlooking Larrimore's house and was munching a sandwich when he saw a blue Jaguar pull up outside the Larrimore gates. The light was beginning to fade and wasn't good enough for him to get a good look at the driver.

For the past two days, he and Fay had kept watch but the operation still had remained negative. Lessing's other men were now checking the smaller rooming houses in the City. So far they had drawn blank. Holtz had been alerted. In his turn, he had alerted Radnitz.

'He's got to be found,' Radnitz had said. 'This is your responsibility,' and knowing he could rely on Holtz to achieve the impossible, he dismissed Elliot from his mind.

Orson, tireless and patient, waited. Now this car had pulled up and he stiffened to attention.

'Here's something,' he said, putting down his sandwich.

Fay joined him at the window and they both examined the car through their field glasses.

'New York plates,' Fay said. 'It can't be Elliot.'

'Look who's here ... the girl,' Orson said. He had spotted Judy running down the drive. 'Alert Fred!'

While Fay was speaking to Nisson on the transceiver, Orson watched Judy get into the Jaguar. There was a moment's pause, then the car drove off, heading towards the centre of the City.

Orson was relieved to see Nisson's Chevy appear and follow the Jaguar.

'Well, how's Superman?' Judy asked as she settled herself beside Vin. 'What's the programme for tonight?'

He glanced at her. She was wearing a red mini skirt, a yellow see through blouse, yellow tights and slippers. He thought she looked pretty good and he said so.

'Low-Life Club,' he told her. 'Let's turn it on there and then we'll go back to that beach you took me to last time.'

'Oh no, we don't! If you're thinking of screwing me on sand you have another thing coming. If you plan to get laid, we'll go to the motel.'

Vin laughed.

'Okay. What have you been doing with yourself?'

She grimaced.

'The usual. I'm sick of the way I'm living! Time's running out. In another two years I'll be twenty! I've got to get some money!'

'I'm not stopping you. Thought any more about those stamps?'

'Yes ... have you?'

'Sure. I think we can swing it, but let's not talk now. Let's have a drink, eat, and then we'll go to the Blue Heaven and make a night of it.'

After an excellent meal, they danced for an hour or so, then Vin said, 'Come on ... let's go.'

Nisson followed them without difficulty to the Blue Heaven motel, watched them check in and go to one of the cabins, then he called Orson.

'They've shacked up at the Blue Heaven motel, Harry,' he reported. 'Want me to stay with them?'

'See if you can find out who he is, Fred.'

'I've got that from his licence tag.' Nissan read off the details he had jotted down which Orson noted.

'Can you get into the cabin next to theirs? I'd like to hear what they're talking about.'

'No can do. The cabins either side are occupied. Besides, from the look of them, there's not going to be much talking.'

'Okay. It's early yet. There's a chance they won't spend the whole night there. Stick around until 02.00, then if there's still no sign of them I'll send a relief and you can go home.'

'Go ... where?' Nisson said bitterly. 'Since when have I a home?'

Orson passed the details he had got on Vin to Lessing who in his turn telexed the PBL Washington for an immediate report back.

Oblivious of this activity, Vin was occupied with Judy. When they had had enough lovemaking, Vin got off the bed, made two stiff whiskies and then returning to the bed he gave his attention to business.

'With your help, baby,' he said, 'I'm sure I can get those stamps, but there are things I must know and you can tell me. You say there's an electric switch that controls all the drawers and the switch is in a steel box let in the wall of the stamp room and kept locked. Right?'

Judy nodded.

'I want you to find out the name of the maker of the steel box. Lock makers are so proud of their safes they invariably have their name on the door. Do you think you can do that?'

'If it's there I can.'

'The same applies to the burglar alarm. There's certain to be a fuse box somewhere in the house. Find out where it is and see if the maker's name is on the box. You say there's a close circuit TV covering the stamp room?'

'Yes. It was installed by Security Guards and the monitor is in their office.'

Vin nodded. 'I know the system. In a city like this it would be popular. They have a big room where screens are hooked to cameras protecting people's homes and one guard watches all the screens. It works pretty well.' He paused to think. 'How come your old man thought of installing a system like that?'

'They have one at the City Hall covering the Kennedy memorial. My old man saw it and fell for it.'

'Why should they have a scanner in the City Hall?'

Judy giggled. 'A year ago, some joker splashed paint on the statue. The City Hall blew its cool and had one installed. Why should they worry ... it's the tax payers' money.'

Vin filed this piece of information away in his mind.

'Your old man keeps the door to the stamp room locked?'

'You bet.'

'How about the windows?'

'When he's not there, there are steel shutters to every window.'

'Is the lock on the door something special?'

'I wouldn't know.'

'Okay, baby, that's something you find out. Do you think you could get hold of the key?'

'Not a hope.'

Seeing she was getting bored with his questions, Vin began to wonder if she was going to be as helpful as he had hoped.

'When does he play golf?'

'Every Tuesday afternoon.'

'Could you get me into the house when he's at the club?'

'Not a hope.'

He resisted an urge to slap her.

'Why not?'

'The lousy staff are always fiddling around. Anyway they wouldn't let you in. I'm not allowed to take my friends home.'

'Use your head,' Vin said impatiently. 'There must be some way you can get me in. How about at night? How do you get in with the alarms set? Don't tell me your old man sits up for you.'

'I have my own entrance. The door from my apartment to the house is always locked after ten o'clock.'

Vin got off the bed.

'I'll take a shower.'

While standing under the cold water, he turned over in his mind the information Judy had given him. When he returned to the bedroom, he said, 'Get dressed. We have work to do.'

'Oh, for God's sake.' Judy squirmed down in the bed. 'I want to sleep. Look at the time!'

Vin was putting on his clothes.

'Never mind about the time. Get dressed!'

Grumbling, she got out of bed and pulled on her panties.

'You know something, Superman?' she said, struggling into her see through blouse, 'you're beginning to bore me.'

'That's too bad.' Vin was now dressed and was writing on a pad he had brought with him. 'Does a million bucks bore you too?'

He tore the page off the pad and gave it to her.

'A reminder. I want all this information tomorrow night. I'll pick you up at the house at nine.'

She read what he had written.

'Okay ... I don't promise anything.'

'I want this information!' Vin snapped. 'You're in this for a million ... so work for it!'

She was startled to see the cold hardness in his eyes.

'Well, don't shout at me.'

'Now I want you to draw a plan of the house.'

Her eyes widened. 'So you're really going to try?'

'That's it, baby,' he said staring intently at her. 'I'm really going to try.'

*   *   *

Soon after 11.00 the following morning, Lessing came briskly into Holtz's office.

'I've found Elliot,' he announced as he shut the door.

'About time.' Holtz was always grudging with praise. 'I'll tell Mr Radnitz. He may want this direct from you.'

Lessing stiffened. Radnitz scared him.

'Don't do that. I ...'

But Holtz had already gone out on to the terrace and a moment later he returned and beckoned to Lessing.

Lessing approached Radnitz like a mouse approaching a cat. Radnitz was reading a document and Lessing waited, his sweating hands gripped tightly behind his back.

Abruptly Radnitz put down the document and stared at Lessing, his eyes hooded.

'Where did you find Elliot?' he asked.

'He is staying at the Seagull, Seaview Boulevard, sir: a small, four bedroom bungalow that is rented to people on vacation.'

'Who owns it?'

'A Mrs Miller of Miami.'

'Did Elliot rent it from her?'

Lessing was thankful he had made thorough inquiries before reporting to Radnitz.

'No, sir. A man called Joe Luck rents it from her. He has rented it for the season now for the past three years. He is living there with his daughter and a man called Vin Pinna.'

'Elliot is living with these three?'

'It would seem so.' Lessing went on to explain how his men had seen Pinna meet Judy Larrimore, how they had followed them to the Blue Heaven motel and then had followed Pinna to the bungalow. 'A watch was kept on the bungalow and at 09.00 Elliot came into the back garden which is screened from the road. He was joined by the other three and they had breakfast together.'

'Who are these three?'

'We have no information as yet on Luck or his daughter, but Pinna has a record. I have an FBI report on him, sir. He is an expert lock man, has served three years for robbery but is not wanted right now.'

Radnitz nodded. 'I want a watch kept on Elliot and on these other three. I want a daily report. On no account are they to know they are being watched ... understood?'

'Yes, sir,' Lessing said, thinking this was easier said than done.

'I want a watch kept on Claude Kendrick. Elliot may contact him. Keep a watch on Larrimore's house and also continue to watch his daughter.'

Realizing the profit he was going to make from this operation, Lessing put on his most efficient air.

'I'll take care of it, sir.'

Radnitz regarded him. His hooded eyes were like tiny pools of ice.

'If there is one mistake, Lessing,' he said, his voice soft, 'then even I will be sorry for you.'

He picked up the document and again began to study it.

Shaken, Lessing looked hopefully at Holtz who ignored him, then he went quickly from the terrace to where Ko-Yu, giving him a sly little grin, opened the front door.

*　　*　　*

Fred Nisson and Alec Ross were men of considerable experience in tailing suspects. They worked together: one in front of the suspect and the other behind. They had an efficient set of signals with which they communicated with each other. To look at they were just a couple of middle aged men on vacation who were wandering around the City, gaping at shop windows, wandering around the stores and being generally harmless.

At 10.30, they saw Joey and Cindy leave the bungalow and drive off in the Jaguar. Both men were startled to see Cindy apparently had become heavily pregnant. Having seen her in the garden an hour ago having breakfast this abrupt transformation foxed them.

'Think it's her twin sister?' Ross asked as he drove after the Jaguar.

'Can't be anything else,' Nisson returned. 'It looks the same girl, but goddamn it, she can't be. This one looks as if she's going to lay an egg any minute.'

Still baffled, they followed the Jaguar into the big parking lot of the Central Self Service store and both men separated, one going ahead of Joey and Cindy, the other lagging behind.

If it had been anyone else but Joey, Nisson and Ross would have been just two men in a crowd, but Joey had a built in antenna that warned him of danger.

The antenna began to quiver as he walked with Cindy into the store. Immediately he looked to right and left to see if there was a store detective around, but he couldn't see one.

Cindy was planning to cook a beef stew and she made her way briskly to the meat counter.

A balding man wearing a blue and white shirt and blue slacks moved on ahead of her. Joey eyed his back and his antenna really came alive.

He touched Cindy's arm. 'No operation, honey,' he said softly. 'I've got a feeling ...' During the years of going around with her father, Cindy had come to respect his 'feelings'. Once she had ignored his warning and they had narrowly escaped disaster. A store detective had been lurking out of sight and it was only because Cindy appeared to be so heavily pregnant that he didn't take action, but told them to get out fast. So now when her father said 'No operation', she obeyed.

They bought what they wanted and while Cindy joined the queue at the paying station, Joey walked through the barrier and waited for her. While he waited, he looked around. The man in the blue and white shirt had bought a bottle of Coke and was standing immediately behind Cindy. Joey's antenna fluttered and he looked away.

Together Cindy and he walked back to the Jaguar.

'I think we're being tailed,' Joey said. 'Take the car. I'll go over to the kiosk and buy cigarettes. You circle for a few minutes, then pick me up at the kiosk.'

Cindy got into the Jaguar and drove away. Joey wandered slowly across the parking lot, pausing to examine a Capri as if the car interested him. He saw the man in the blue and white shirt driving after Cindy. But his antenna still fluttered and he felt sure there was a second tail watching him. He went over to the kiosk and bought a pack of cigarettes and also the *Paradise Herald*. He paused to scan the headlines, then glanced around but there were so many people that he was unable to spot the second taller although he was sure he was there.

He continued to appear to be reading the paper until the Jaguar pulled in to the parking lot. Joey got in and Cindy drove off.

'Where to, dad?' she asked.

Joey shifted the driving mirror so he could watch the cars behind. He saw another nondescript looking man wearing a green shirt get in the car beside the man in the blue and white shirt and the car moved after them.

'We are being tailed,' Joey said, his voice unsteady. 'They don't look like cops, but they could be private eyes. Keep going. We'll go up into the hills and see if they really mean business.'

'Why should they be tailing us?' Cindy asked, her eyes growing round.

'I don't know and I don't like it.'

Once free of the heavy traffic, Cindy put on speed and turning off the highway, she took a side road that led up into the hills. After a minute or so, Joey again checked the driving mirror. There was no sign of the following car.

'Keep going,' he said. 'I think we've lost them, but they could be foxing.'

In the following car, Ross cursed softly as he saw the Jaguar turn off the highway.

'I think they've spotted us, Fred,' he said. 'If I go up that road after them, they'll know for sure they are being tailed.' He pulled into a lay-by. 'How the hell did they get on to us?'

Nisson, acutely aware of Lessing's instructions that the suspects were on no account to know they were being tailed, broke out in a gentle sweat.

'I don't understand it, but I think you're right. Let's get back to the bungalow. From now on, Alec, we've got to be a damn sight more careful with these people. Maybe I'd better report to the old man.'

'And get chewed to hell? We don't know for sure they did spot us. Let's wait and see how it works out.'

130

When Joey was sure they had lost the following car, he told Cindy to take the loop road that would bring them back on to the highway.

'We'll go home,' Joey said. 'Don will want to know about this.'

When Joey told Elliot he stared in disbelief.

'Are you sure?'

'I wouldn't swear to it, but I think so.'

'Well, let's take it they were tailing you,' Elliot said. 'They could only be tailing you because they suspect you have been helping yourselves in the various stores. Why else should they tail you? Now listen, from now on, we pay for everything we want ... understand? We don't want you two arrested on a shop lifting charge just when we are starting this operation.' He turned to Vin who had been listening and frowning. 'You too, Vin. Keep your eyes skinned just in case these two men are also interested in you. If you think you are being tailed, act normally. Don't try to lose the tailer. The time to start losing them is when we go for the stamps.'

'But why should they be tailing us?' Joey asked. 'These two weren't cops. I can smell a cop a mile away.'

'Could they have been store detectives?'

'I don't think so ... maybe they could have been, but I reckon I know all the store dicks by sight in this City and don't tell me store dicks would follow us in a car.'

Elliot shrugged. 'Anyway, you think you lost them?'

'No question about that.'

'Okay, watch it ... let's all watch it. Maybe it was a false alarm.'

*　　*　　*

131

That night Vin picked Judy up outside the Larrimore house. Conscious of Elliot's warning, he checked several times in his driving mirror to make sure he wasn't being followed.

Nisson, much more careful now, had got a second car. While Ross drove ahead of Vin, Nisson, in the second car, kept in touch with Ross by a transceiver and followed Vin by using the side streets.

As soon as Vin pulled up to let Judy get into the car, Nisson alerted Orson, watching from the empty villa and Orson told him in which direction Vin was driving. In this way Nisson was able to follow Vin without being spotted to the Coq d'Or restaurant.

Vin was feeling good. As soon as Judy had got into the Jaguar he had asked her if she had the information he wanted and she said she had.

'Fine baby ... I'll buy you an expensive dinner.'

Judy refused to tell him what she had found out until the dinner was ordered. Then while waiting for the lobster soufflé she handed him the sheet of paper on which he had written the reminders for her and he saw she had scribbled in the answers.

He studied the information and nodded his satisfaction. He now had the name of the firm who had installed the burglar alarms and also the name of the people who had arranged the electric switch controlling the drawers that contained the stamps. He knew both these firms and he knew just how to handle their appliances. This would be easier than he had thought.

'This is fine, baby,' he said and called for a bottle of champagne.

Judy regarded him.

'Does this mean something to you?'

'Sure ... sure.' He grinned. 'It means we are that much closer to those stamps and to all that lovely bread.'

'But how are you going to find the stamps?'

He patted her hand. 'I'll find them.'

Later, both feeling relaxed with the good food, Judy said, 'I feel like being screwed. Let's go to the Blue Heaven.'

'Not tonight, baby,' Vin said. 'We're going to your pad.'

She stiffened.

'That's something we don't do!'

'Come on, baby.' Vin signalled for the bill. 'We're in business ... remember? I want to take a look at the lock on your door to the house.'

'You're crazy! I'm not taking you home!'

He smiled at her. Settling the bill with the money Elliot had given him, he got to his feet.

'Let's go.'

Nisson on his transceiver alerted Ross that the Jaguar was heading his way. Ross set his car rolling and in a few moments, he saw the Jaguar's headlights in his driving mirror. He kept going.

Seeing the direction in which Vin was driving, Nisson guessed he was taking Judy home. He told Ross to speed up and get to the house before Vin did.

Vin pulled up outside the Larrimore gates, cut the engine and got out of the car.

'Come on, baby ... let's go,' he said.

Judy hesitated, then getting out of the car, she went with him up the drive towards the house.

Through night glasses, Orson watched with interest.

As they neared the house, Vin paused in the shade of a flowering shrub. There were lights showing on the top floor: the second floor was in darkness and a single light showed on the ground floor.

133

'What gives?' he asked. 'What are those lights?'

'The staff on the top floor and the stamp room on the ground floor,' Judy told him.

He had memorized the plan she had drawn of the house, but he wanted to be sure. Pointing to the far wing of the house, he asked, 'That's where you are?'

'Yes.'

Taking her arm, he walked with her across the lawn, keeping in the shadows until they reached the entrance to her rooms. She unlocked the door and they went in.

'I want to take a look at that lock.'

She led him through a small sitting-room to a lobby.

'That's it,' she said and pointed.

He examined the lock and grinned.

'Strictly for kids,' he said. 'Fine ... okay, baby, I'll get moving. See you tomorrow night, huh?'

'Well, since you forced your way in ... you'd better stay.'

'No ... the Jag out there's too much of an ad. See you nine o'clock tomorrow night. I'll take you to the Adam and Eve club ... okay?'

'But it's only eleven o'clock,' Judy protested. 'I'll come with you. Let's go to the club now.'

'Sorry, baby ... I've got business. Tomorrow, we'll have a ball,' and he left her.

*   *   *

While Vin and Judy were at the Coq d'Or restaurant, Elliot and Cindy were in the garden of the bungalow and Joey was watching TV.

Elliot had never felt more relaxed. Cindy had seen his stump and had actually cradled it in her hands and she had cried a little. By her attitude and by the way she had insisted on taking the stump in her hands Elliot now no longer felt he was some goddamn crippled freak. He knew as he had watched her he could make love to her and she would have given herself willingly, but he hesitated. He had asked her bluntly if she had ever made love and Cindy, blushing, had admitted she hadn't.

Now, seated side by side, looking at the yellow moon, Elliot took her hand.

'You mean a lot to me, Cindy,' he said. 'I believe I'm half in love with you and I get the idea it's the same with you, but it won't work. I'm not for you. There's something fatal about me. I've never brought anyone any happiness, least of all myself. I'm telling you this because I don't want you to get hurt.'

'I won't get hurt. I love you and that's that,' Cindy said, not looking at him. 'I've loved you from the moment I met you.'

He shook his head despondently.

'I've got no future to share with you. You know something? You're dead without money.' He let go of her hand. 'That may seem a crazy thing to say, but it's true. I don't mean that you or Joey are dead without money ... but I am. I've always thought this way. Life means nothing to me without the things, the power, the service that money can buy. That's the way I'm made. If it wasn't for you and all the process servers after me I couldn't have stayed in this mean little house for ten minutes. But just having you around and the thought that with luck I'll pick up a lump of money has made it possible. When I get that money I'm going to have a final splash and it's going to be one hell of a splash.'

'But with a hundred thousand dollars,' Cindy said quietly, 'you can live well for a long time, Don. With me to help out, you could live ...'

He laughed. 'We're on the wrong wavelength, Cindy. I don't want to live a long time ... I'm tired of living ... like

135

ol' man River.' He made an impatient movement. 'I'm talking too much. I just want you to know that after this job we're going to say goodbye. I want you to put me right out of your mind as I intend to put you out of my mind ... that way no one gets hurt.'

He broke off abruptly as Vin and Joey came out of the bungalow and moved towards them.

Vin dropped into a nearby chair while Joey sat on the grass.

'My part of the operation is fixed,' Vin said. 'I've got all the info I need from the chick to get at the stamps except in which drawer they're kept. No trouble at all. The alarms can be fixed. There's just one problem but this can also be fixed. This is where Joey pulls his weight.'

Cindy heard Vin's voice, but she didn't hear what he was saying. Her mind was far away, thinking of what Elliot had just said to her. She felt a pang of misery. There had been something in his quiet voice that warned her he had meant what he said. How could she ever put him out of her mind?

But if Cindy wasn't listening, Elliot was.

'What's the problem?'

'There's a TV scanner in the stamp room,' Vin said. 'Judy has shown me on her plan where it is. It revolves in a semicircle, sweeping the room, but by keeping on my hands and knees I can keep out of its range. But the snag is I have to get into the room by the door. Even if I crawl in, the guard watching the monitor would see the door open even if he didn't see me. It'll take me around three seconds to open the door, get into the room and then close the door. In those three seconds I could be spotted. Now the system works like this. All Security Guard scanners are hooked to monitors in their headquarters: there are around forty monitors to a room and a guard sits watching them. If he sees something on one of the monitors he doesn't like he presses a button on the monitor that alerts a patrol car that goes at once to investigate.'

'Never mind the system,' Joey said uneasily. 'Where do I come in on this?'

'You cause a diversion.'

'What does that mean?'

'You know the Kennedy memorial at the City Hall?'

Joey blinked. 'Yes ... what's that to do with this?'

'Once a practical joker splashed paint on it and since then it has been protected by a Security Guard scanner. The City Hall is pretty touchy about the memorial ... it cost them a lot of dough. Now your job is to look as if you're going to damage the statue ... you don't of course, but you look as if you might be going to do something. When the guard spots you on the monitor, he isn't going to be looking at Larrimore's monitor. If we time it to a split second, I can get the door open, get in, shut the door, get the stamps and get out again while the guard is watching you, trying to make up his mind whether to alert the patrol car or not.' Vin looked at Elliot. 'What do you think?'

'It's a good idea, but it's certainly got to be timed right.'

'What happens to me if the cops pick me up?' Joey asked uneasily.

'Nothing,' Elliot said gently. 'You don't have to worry about that. The way I see it: you're on vacation. You are a Kennedy fan and you've got a little drunk. You want to pay a tribute to him. You have a bottle of Scotch with you. What nicer thought than to leave the bottle at the foot of the statue? Maybe the cops will treat you a little rough, but they'll let you go once they see you're harmless. Yes ... it's a great idea ... it'll work.'

137

Vin sat back, grinning. 'You see? I've buttoned my end up, now it's up to you and Cindy to button your end up. Get me the number of the drawer and I'll get the stamps.'

'There's one of your buttons left undone,' Elliot said quietly. 'Has Judy told you the name of the buyer?'

Vin's smug smile slipped.

'Not yet. When I get the stamps, she'll tell me.'

'Can you trust her?'

Vin stiffened. 'What does that mean?'

'You said she wanted a thousand dollars. She could give you any name, couldn't she?'

'You take me for a dope? She has agreed in return for a grand to give me the letter this guy wrote to her old man offering to buy the stamps,' Vin said hotly. 'That covers us, doesn't it?'

'Suppose this buyer has changed his mind by now?'

'To hell with that for an idea! But suppose he has changed his mind, then we sell the stamps to Kendrick. Okay, we don't make so much, but we make something.'

Elliot nodded.

The following morning, a letter addressed to Cindy was in the mail box. Joey found it and brought it to the breakfast table. All four stared at the neat writing on the envelope.

'This is it,' Elliot said. 'Go ahead, Cindy ... open it.'

Cindy shook her head. 'You open it, Don.'

Elliot slit open the envelope, extracted a sheet of notepaper and read the few lines. His eyes lit up with excitement.

'It's worked! Larrimore will see you tomorrow morning at eleven!' He tossed the letter on the table.

When they had all read it, Vin said, 'Okay, now it's up to you, baby. For Pete's sake, don't louse it up!'

'She won't.' Elliot smiled at Cindy. 'You've got to dress the part. Buy yourself a simple cotton dress; make yourself look as young as you can ... fix your hair. You're just a small time kid left something by her grandfather and you're hoping it's worth a fortune.'

Tense, her eyes wide, Cindy nodded.

Elliot regarded her.

'It doesn't scare you?'

'No, but if he hasn't the book on him ...'

'He lives with it,' Vin broke in. 'Judy swears he's never without it.'

'All right, then I can get it, but I may not have a chance to look at it. He may not leave me long enough for me to find the entry ... that really worries me.'

'Yes.' Elliot nodded. 'That's the gamble. Let's see if we can shorten the odds.' He thought for a moment. 'Suppose I telephone him while you are with him? When he answers the phone you can check the book. How's that?'

'But suppose I haven't been able to get the book before you phone? You won't know when I've got it.'

'That's right.' Elliot reached for a cigarette while he considered this, then he snapped his fingers. 'A walkie talkie! Joey, get one: small and powerful. Cindy has one in her bag. I'll be waiting here with the other.' He looked at Cindy. 'All you have to do when you've got the book is to open your bag and say into it "Okay." I'll then call Larrimore.'

'That's fixed it,' Vin said, getting to his feet. 'Come on, Joey, I'll drive you down town.'

When they had gone, Elliot said, 'If you get the drawer number, Cindy, don't tell Vin. If we tell him, we'll have no hold on him. He could sneak out of here, get the stamps, do a deal with Larrimore's daughter and leave us high and dry.'

'But he must be told if he is to get the stamps.'

'I'm going with him,' Elliot said. 'It's the only way. When we get into the stamp room, I'll take the stamps and I'll do the selling. Do you know where he keeps his gun?'

139

Cindy's eyes popped wide open.

'No.'

'Must be in his room.' Elliot got up and went into Vin's small bedroom. He found the gun after a search and he unloaded it. A further search produced a box of cartridges. 'I'll dump these,' he said to Cindy who was standing in the doorway, watching him. 'Something tells me Vin would use the gun if he was under pressure.'

'Don ... I wish you wouldn't go with him. Suppose something goes wrong? Suppose you got caught?'

'There's no other way.' Elliot grinned. 'Know something? This is the first real fun I've ever had in my life.'

* * *

The following morning as the hands of the clock on the overmantel moved to 11.00, the three men sat around the table in the living-room of the bungalow. The telephone was in front of Elliot and the walkie talkie, switched on, by the telephone.

Early in the morning, Cindy had walked to Larrimore's house and had tested the two way radio which worked well. She had timed the walk and found it took her seventeen minutes from the bungalow without hurrying. Satisfied with the test, she returned to the bungalow.

Orson who was catching the early morning stint picked up Cindy's voice and Elliot's answering voice on his transceiver. As Cindy had only said 'Okay' and Elliot had only replied 'Hear you,' then had switched off, Orson was puzzled.

'They're cooking up something,' he said to Fay who was heating coffee. 'I'd better alert the old man.'

'At this time, he should love that,' Fay said.

But Orson went to the telephone that Lessing had had laid on and called Lessing at his home. He explained what he had seen and heard.

'Looks like they're going to make a try tonight,' Lessing said. 'They wouldn't start anything until Larrimore has gone to bed. He goes late. I'll get the boys down there around 22.00. If they do start something, we'll catch them as they come out.'

Now, it was approaching D-hour. Joey was pale and sweating. Vin, uneasy, couldn't keep his eyes off the clock. Elliot seemed completely relaxed.

As the hands of the clock moved to eleven, he said, 'She's arrived.'

'Suppose the punk won't see her?' Vin said. 'That would really sink us.'

'I know Larrimore. He'll see her. I told her not to part with the stamp album to a servant.' Elliot looked at Joey. 'What's worrying you? You haven't lost confidence in her, have you?'

Joey shook his head.

'She'll get the book if it's on him, but it's finding the drawer number ...' He mopped his sweating face. 'Suppose he spots her? What would he do?'

'He'd kick her out,' Elliot said. 'He wouldn't send for the police if that's what's worrying you. That I'm sure of.'

That was all that was worrying Joey. The thought of his beloved Cindy being taken away by a cop made him feel ill, but Elliot's reassuring voice helped him a lot.

The minutes crept by.

At 11.15, Vin muttered an expletive.

'She isn't going to get it! Now what the hell are we going to do?'

'Shut up!' Elliot snapped. He also found himself growing tense. 'You don't expect her to get it the moment she meets him, do you?'

Vin growled and lit another cigarette.

141

At 11.40, even Elliot was beginning to sweat. Joey was in such a state, he had to hold his handkerchief to his face while Vin was now pacing up and down the small room.

Suddenly he stopped pacing. His eyes vicious with rage, he exclaimed, 'She's loused it up! I never did think she would do it! She hadn't the guts to go through with it!'

'Shut your big mouth,' Elliot snapped, 'or do you want me to shut it for you?'

Vin glared at him.

'You and who else ... tin foot?'

As Elliot made to stand up, Joey put a restraining hand on his arm.

'Don ... please ... this isn't the time.'

Then clearly and distinctly, Cindy's voice, coming from the receiver set, said, 'Okay.'

The three men stared at each other, not quite sure if they had heard right.

'Did you hear that?' Elliot demanded.

'It was Cindy,' Joey said.

'Yeah.' Vin came to the table. 'She's done it!'

With a slightly unsteady hand, Elliot picked up the telephone receiver and dialled Larrimore's number. There was a delay, then a man's voice said, 'Mr Larrimore's residence.'

'This is Don Elliot calling Mr Larrimore.'

'Mr Larrimore is engaged at the moment, sir. Shall I ask him to call you back?'

'I want to speak to him right away. Tell him I'd be obliged if he would come to the phone.'

There was more delay, then Larrimore came on the line. Elliot recognized his voice as he said, 'Is that you, Elliot?'

'Hello there. I'm sorry to interrupt something. Your man said you were tied up.'

'Yes ... I am rather occupied. How are you, Elliot? I haven't seen or heard from you for months.'

At least, Elliot thought, Larrimore sounded cordial.

'I've been recouping. You heard about the accident?'

'Of course. I'm very sorry.'

'One of those things, but I've now got on top of my tin foot. How about a game on Tuesday? I've shortened my swing and reduced my pivot and I'm playing better than ever. You might try that, Larrimore. A short swing gives you much more control.'

'That's an idea. Yes, let's have a game. I'm so glad you are playing again. My congratulations. Then Tuesday at three o'clock?'

'That's a date.' Elliot chit chatted about the Stock market prices, determined to give Cindy all the time she needed, then finally, he hung up. He drew in a deep breath. 'She must have got the number by now.'

It wasn't until 12.45 that the three waiting men saw Cindy come up the garden path and they jumped to their feet and rushed to her, Elliot slightly in the lead.

She looked pale and he could see she was a little shaky, but she smiled at him as he asked, 'Did you get it?'

'Yes.'

'Come on in … let's hear about it,' Elliot said, putting his arm around her. 'Well done! I was sure you would succeed!'

'What's the drawer number?' Vin demanded, crowding up behind them as they entered the sitting-room.

'She's not telling you that, Vin,' Elliot said and he pushed Cindy gently away from him so he faced Vin.

Joey, standing in the doorway, stared first at Cindy and then at Elliot, his eyes growing round.

'Who says?' Vin snarled. 'I've as much right to know as you have! Get out of my way! I'll talk to her!'

'Relax,' Elliot said. 'When you give me the name of the buyer, I'll give you the number of the drawer. Do you think we three are dopes? None of us trust you, Vin. Your double cross isn't going to jell.'

Vin's eyes narrowed.

'Double cross? What the hell do you mean?'

'Don't let's waste time. Get the name of the buyer. I'll give you a thousand dollars for Judy. Get the name tonight then you and I will go to Larrimore's house and get the stamps, but I'm going to deal with the buyer.'

For a long moment, Vin stood staring at Elliot. This was so unexpected, his brain couldn't cope with it. Controlling his fury, and realizing he would have to give himself time to think, he shrugged.

'Okay, okay, no one's asking you to trust me. I'll get the buyer's name, but you don't come with me, buster. This is a job for experts and I don't work with amateurs.'

'Get the name,' Elliot said quietly, 'then we'll talk about the rest of it.'

Vin looked at Cindy. 'Are you going to tell me the number, baby?'

Cindy shook her head.

Vin grinned evilly at her.

'Sure? You'd better be sure. You could be sorry later.'

She stared at him unflinchingly.

'I'm sure.'

'Okay.'

He turned and walked out of the bungalow and down to his car.

'We'd better tell him,' Joey said fearfully. 'He could do something to Cindy.'

'We don't have to tell him,' Cindy said and opened her bag. 'I've got the stamps.'

7

There was a long moment of silence as Elliot and Joey watched Cindy take a plastic envelope from her bag and lay it on the table.

'These are the stamps, aren't they?'

His heart beating fast, his breathing uneven, Elliot looked at the eight stamps through their plastic cover. He recognized them immediately from the photocopy that Kendrick had shown him.

'Yes.' His voice was husky. He straightened and looked at Cindy. 'Why did you take them, you crazy kid? As soon as Larrimore finds they are missing, he'll call the police. They'll come here! We wrote to him and he knows this address! What were you thinking of?'

'I don't think he will call the police,' Cindy said.

'Why do you say that?'

She sat down abruptly and looked so pale, Joey rushed to the liquor cabinet and began to pour a brandy.

'No, daddy ... I don't want it,' she protested. 'I'm all right.' Joey regarded her, stared at the brandy in the glass and then swallowed it himself.

'Why do you say he won't tell the police?' Elliot repeated, sitting at the table and facing her.

'There was a letter in the drawer with the stamps,' Cindy told him. 'It was from the Central Intelligence Agency, Washington. It said it was an offence to have these stamps

145

and the owner would be prosecuted if he didn't notify the CIA if he had them. The letter was dated two months ago. They said the maximum sentence would be three years and a fine of thirty thousand dollars. When I read that I saw Mr Larrimore couldn't complain to the police without getting into trouble so I took them.'

'The CIA?' Elliot's voice shot up a note.

'Yes.'

'Suppose you tell us just what happened, Cindy.'

She drew in a deep breath, then said, 'I arrived at the house and Mr Larrimore took me into the stamp room. He was nice and kind. He told me to sit down and he looked through the stamp album. The only stamps that interested him were the ones dad had bought. He said they might be worth three hundred dollars. Then just as I was wondering how I could get the index from him, he took it from his pocket and looked at it. Then he took me over to one of the drawers and showed me other stamps in the same series as the ones in the album. He left the book on his desk. It was so easy. He asked me if I would leave the stamp album with him. I got a little behind him, opened my bag and gave you the signal. Then you phoned. He excused himself and left me in the room. I found the drawer number in the index. I could hear him talking to you so I went to the drawer and found the stamps. Then I saw the letter. He was still talking to you so I read it. It seemed to me that if I took the stamps he couldn't call the police ... so I took them.'

'For Pete's sake!' Elliot leaned forward and took her hand. 'That was quick thinking, but he could tell the police.'

'I don't think he will,' Cindy said. 'Anyway, it's worth the risk, Now, you don't have to break in.'

'You shouldn't have done it,' Joey said, his voice quavering. 'You should have left it to Don and Vin.'

'We have them,' Cindy said.

146

'We can't keep them here.' Elliot paused to think. 'Joey, take them right away to the Chase National Bank. Buy an envelope, write your name on it and put the stamps in it. Rent a safe deposit box. Get going, Joey! If the police come here and find them we're sunk.'

Joey nodded. Picking up the plastic envelope he put it in his pocket.

'What shall I do with the key?'

'Bring it back here. We'll hide it some place.'

When Joey had gone, Elliot regarded Cindy.

'You shouldn't have done it, Cindy.'

She smiled at him.

'I just couldn't bear the thought of you going with Vin into that house. Vin's dangerous. Once he got the stamps, he might have done something to you.'

'But why is the CIA interested?' Elliot said. 'Was it a personal letter to Larrimore?'

'It was a circular letter addressed to philatelists.'

'And it said it was an offence to hold the stamps?'

'Yes.'

Elliot didn't like this.

'I don't understand it, but it looks as if the temptation to keep such rare stamps was too much for Larrimore.' He thought, then nodded. 'Yes, I think you're right. He would be asking for trouble if he complained to the police.' He stared uneasily at Cindy. 'But why the CIA?'

'Perhaps we'd better not try to sell them,' Cindy said.

'They're safe for the moment. Let's find out who the buyer is before we make up our minds. And not a word about this to Vin.' Elliot got up and coming around the table, he put his arms around her.

'You've done a marvellous job, Cindy.'

She put her head against his shoulder and clung to him.

*　　*　　*

147

Barney had been talking now non stop, apart from eating and drinking, for the past two hours The time was after 23.00 and the Neptune bar was now lined with fishermen, noisy in their demands for beer and Sam, the barman, was being kept busy.

Barney paused to regard the backs of the men as they leaned on the bar and his fat face wore an expression of disapproval.

'Fishermen!' he said scornfully. 'No good riff raff. You take my word for it, Mr Campbell. They spend all their nights drinking when they should be home keeping their wives and children company.'

I asked him if he was married.

'I know better, mister,' he said. 'The thing I object to about marriage is a guy never gets a chance to talk and if there's one thing I like – excluding beer – it's talking.'

I said I could understand that.

'Yeah.' He paused to wave his empty glass in Sam's direction. 'You take these men over there. All they think about is money, women and drinking. I've never been mercenary. If you offered me a million dollars I wouldn't take it. I wouldn't know what to do with it. What the hell does a man want with a million dollars?'

I could have told him, but I got the impression he wouldn't be interested. He paused while Sam rushed a beer to his table, then went on, 'But this Vin Pinna I'm telling you about had the itch to get his hands on this million Judy Larrimore had told him about. He had the itch the same way as a dog gets the itch for a lady dog every now and again if you'll excuse the comparison. Now Vin had been brought up in a tough world. I don't say he didn't know better, but knowing better and doing better are two different things ... right, Mr Campbell?'

I said that was indisputable.

'Well, when he realized that Elliot wasn't going to give him the number of the drawer and also had said he would go to the buyer himself, Vin decided Elliot had to be got rid of. He had driven to the cliff head and was sitting in the Jaguar and he gave his mind to the problem. He decided after getting his brain to work – and this was a slow process because up to now Vin seldom used his brain – that the only way he could get his hands on all this money was just to find out from Judy who the buyer was, then get rid of Elliot, then scare Cindy into telling him the number of the drawer.

'For perhaps five or six minutes, Vin hesitated about getting rid of Elliot. Up to now he had kept clear of murder. Once or twice, when he had been disturbed by a householder while he was robbing a safe, he had been tempted, but he found by threatening the householder with a gun, murder hadn't been necessary. But, thinking about the past, he did see that if the householder had turned awkward he would have pulled the trigger.

'Turning all this over in his sluggish mind, Vin came to the conclusion that for a million dollars he would commit not one murder but several if anyone tried to outsmart him. For that sum of money, he would take murder in his stride.

'Having got that little problem solved, he turned his mind to Judy. It was no good knocking Elliot off without first knowing who the buyer was. Judy was a tricky chick. She had already told him that she wasn't giving him the name of the buyer until he got the stamps and even when he had them she was doing the deal with the buyer. This meant he would be lucky if she didn't gyp him out of the two hundred and fifty thousand she had promised him.

'This was pretty frustrating to Vin because he had no intention of taking that kind of money when he could get a million if he worked at it.'

A massively built man, wearing a dirty sweat shirt and oil stained white ducks, knots of black hair on his arms, shoulders and chest, came into the bar. He was around twenty-five years of age, his ugly face good natured and he was hailed by the other men standing up at the bar with a warmth that told me he was a bar favourite.

He spotted Barney and waved to him.

'Hi, Fat-guts!' he bellowed in a voice that made my eardrums quiver, 'having a ball?'

Barney didn't deign to look his way.

'He will come to no good, Mr Campbell,' he said as soon as the massive man had been absorbed in the crowd. 'No respect for his elders or his betters ... just a low fisherman. Fat-guts! Wait till he's my age. Like I said ... no respect.'

I said that was the trouble with the younger generation.

'You're right, Mr Campbell.' Barney sipped his beer. 'Well, getting back to Vin ... he sat in the car and wondered how he was going to handle Judy. The more he thought about her the more irritated he got. Now when a thug like Vin gets irritated, he becomes like a vicious dog. Sooner or later the dog will snap and then bite and Vin was built on the same lines. He decided he would force Judy to give him the name of this stamp buyer. He would scare her into opening her mouth even if he had to rough her up. Once he had made this decision, he considered how he was going to do it.

'He had no illusions about Judy. She was tricky and he was sure she was tough. Even if he roughed her up so she parted with the buyer's name, as soon as he let her go, she would squeal to the cops. Once the cops moved in, it was goodbye to all that money. Vin thought about this for over half an hour, then he came to the logical solution. If he was going to knock Elliot off, what was the matter with knocking Judy off too? Once rid of her, once rid of Elliot all he had to do was to make Cindy talk and if she got tricky why not knock her off as well? If he had to knock her off, then to make a nice clean job of it, he would also knock off Joey.

'Vin now realized that it was one thing to think about knocking off four people but quite another thing to do it successfully. By successfully, he naturally meant having no trouble with the cops. What was the use of getting a million dollars if you had the cops breathing down your neck?

'He would have four bodies to get rid of ... one was tricky enough ... but four!

'Then he remembered the deserted cove Judy had taken him to the first time they had met. Burying bodies in sand wasn't hard work. Hard work never had appealed to Vin. But he couldn't believe no one ever went to the cove and sooner or later some kid would dig or the sea would wash up and then there would be trouble.

'He thought some more and finally decided that the cove was too dangerous. Then he remembered seeing a bulldozer at work on swamp land a few miles outside the City. He remembered hearing a barman talking about a big reclaiming scheme and another luxury hotel going up there. This might be a hiding place for bodies.

'So Vin drove out to the swamp right away. He found three bulldozers working, tearing up mangrove trees and levelling the ground and a twenty foot high cement mixer grinding out cement which was being used to cover the masses of rubble trucks were unloading.

'Vin sat in the car and watched the cement mixer at work. He noted there was a perpendicular steel ladder going to the top. After a while, he convinced himself that he could carry a body up there and tip it into the mouth of the machine. What better method of getting rid of a body?'

Barney paused and squinted at me.

'From all this, Mr Campbell,' he said, 'you can see how the thought of so much money turns a man into something less than an animal. Once Vin convinced himself that he could get rid of the bodies without trace, he drove away from the swamp feeling pretty pleased with himself. The first move would be to get Judy to part with the buyer's name. He would fix that when he met her this evening. He wondered now how he could kill her quickly, silently and without mess. This was important if he was going to knock her off at the Blue Heaven motel.

'As he drove through the shade of the palm trees that lined the highway, he considered the various methods he had heard about while in jail and while fraternizing with various criminals in New York. A gun or a knife were out: there must be no blood. He considered a crushing blow at the back of the head, but that still might produce blood. He had read somewhere that there was an artery in the neck which, if pressed hard enough, would produce the required effect, but as he had no idea where the artery was located he passed that one over. Then he remembered a Mafia button man he had once met who was a garrotte artist. His garrotte had been a dog lead so if the cops ever searched him and found it, he had an explanation ready. The lead whipped over the head, the hands crossed, a knee driven into the back did the trick in a few seconds.

' "Why not?" Vin said aloud.

'On his way back to the bungalow he stopped at a pet store and bought a leather dog lead.

'The pansy assistant asked him if he would like the name of his dog stamped on the lead.

152

' "You may not believe it," the assistant said, regarding Vin with serious eyes, "but doggies do know and they do care. It won't take a tiny moment and it will be only three dollars extra."

'Vin told him to get stuffed.

'In the meantime, Joey got back to the bungalow. As soon as he came into the back garden, Elliot saw he was worried. He and Cindy had been waiting for Joey's return and as he joined them, Elliot said a little anxiously, "All okay, Joey?"

' "Yes." Joey sat down. "I rented a safe and here's the key." He handed Elliot a safe deposit key. "But we're being tailed, Don. I didn't spot the tailers, but I get a feeling and it's never wrong. I was picked up as soon as I left here. As soon as I got the feeling, I shook the tailer off ... I lost him. It was tricky. He was good, but I lost him."

' "What's going on?" Elliot was puzzled. "That's the second time you think you were followed." Then he remembered that the CIA were interested in the stamps. Could the CIA be following Joey? He decided he wouldn't start a scare without more information so he said nothing. "You're sure you lost them?"

' "I'm sure," Joey said.

'Elliot got to his feet.

' "Suppose we hide the key in the potting shed? Think that's an idea?"

'Joey agreed.

'They went together into the small shed that housed a few gardening tools and a battered power mower. Elliot hid the key under a can of weed killer.

' "Now if anything happens to any of us, those left will know where it is," Elliot said.

'Joey looked sharply at him.

' "What does that mean?"

'Elliot grinned.

' "Probably nothing. Tell Cindy where it's hidden."

'Later, Vin returned to the bungalow. Joey and Cindy had gone for a walk and Vin found Elliot on his own in the garden. "Give me a thousand bucks," Vin said, "and I'll get the buyer's name tonight."

'Elliot studied him.

' "Okay ... you are sure she will tell you?"

' "Yeah."

' "She could be conning you."

'Vin moved impatiently.

' "We've gone over all that jazz. She showed me the letter her old man had from the buyer."

"And you will show it to me?"

' "Sure ... if she'll part with it."

' "Look, Vin, no offence, but I don't trust you. I have to be sure the name of the man you give me is the buyer. Get me his name and I'll call him. If he says he'll buy, I'll give you the number of the drawer, but not before."

'Vin restrained his temper with an effort.

' "Get me the money and stop acting like a goddamn movie star."

' "Just so long as you know," Elliot said and went into the bungalow.

'Vin stared after him, his eyes vicious.'

*　　*　　*

Orson was alerted by Nisson around 21.00 that Pinna in the Jaguar was heading his way. He immediately alerted the six men Lessing had stationed around Larrimore's house: three of them in the garden, two in a parked car and one patrolling the road.

'This could be it,' he said. 'Pinna's on his way. Let him get into the house, then grab him as he comes out. Watch it! He could be armed!'

His mind totally occupied in how he was going to force Judy to tell him the name of the buyer, Vin completely forgot Elliot's warning to watch out that he wasn't being tailed. He was oblivious that Ross was driving ahead of him and Nisson behind him. When he reached Larrimore's house, he pulled up, lit a cigarette and waited for Judy to show.

He would have to be careful not to arouse her suspicions, he told himself. He would take her to the Low-Life Club, give her dinner, then take her to the Blue Heaven motel. Once in the cabin, he would ask her for the buyer's name, then if she didn't come across, he would knock her cold, gag and bind her and see what a few lighted cigarettes applied to her legs would do to get her talking. When she had parted with the name, he would call this guy and ask him if he were interested in buying the stamps. If he was and agreed the price, then Judy would cease to exist.

Although tense, he managed a wide grin as Judy got into the car.

'How about the Low-Life Club, baby?' he asked, shifting into gear, 'then we can go to the Blue Heaven. Okay with you?'

'Fine.' She regarded him. 'How are your plans working out, Superman? Any nearer to the stamps?'

'Yeah. Let's talk about that at the motel ...' Vin said. 'Pleasure before business, huh?'

'You mean you've found out where he keeps them?'

'I didn't say that, but I'm getting nearer.'

'You sound cagey.'

He grinned at her. 'That makes two of us, doesn't it?'

'Is that girl who came to see my old man this morning hooked up with you?'

Vin stiffened and gaped, then realizing she was watching him and he had given himself away, he said, 'That's right. You saw her then?'

'I saw her. What's she to you?'

'Me? She's just a kid ... nothing.'

'She didn't look such a kid to me. Why did the old bastard see her?'

'Okay,' Vin said. 'We'll go to the motel first. I'll tell you and you tell me.'

'What's that mean?'

'You'll see.'

He turned off the highway on to a side road that led to the motel.

'Have you become a dog lover, Superman?' she asked suddenly.

Vin twisted his head to stare at her.

'Dog lover?' Then he stiffened as he saw she was holding the dog lead he had bought and which had been in his pocket. 'Oh that ...' He felt sweat break out on his face.

'Where's the dog?' she asked, staring at him.

'I don't take it around. I've left him in my flat.'

'And little miss prissy looks after him?'

'Nothing like that, baby. He's an old dog. He likes being alone.'

'What kind of dog?'

Vin had no idea what kind of dogs there were since he never bothered about dogs. He shrugged.

'Oh, a dog ... big, floppy ... a dog.'

'What's his name?'

Vin drew in a slow breath of exasperation.

'How the hell ... its name? Joe.'

156

'That's a funny name for a dog.'

'That's what I call him ... you interested in dogs?'

'No.' Again she looked steadily at him as she handled the lead. 'I'm just curious why you should have a dog lead in your pocket.'

'I was late ... didn't want to keep you waiting. I guess I forgot it was in my pocket.' Vin slowed to drive through the archway leading into the motel.

'When I saw this hanging out of your pocket, I got the idea you might be kinky and wanted to beat me with it.' Vin pulled into a parking bay.

'Would you like that?'

'I've never tried it. Maybe.'

He took the lead from her and stuffed it into his pocket.

'I don't dig for that stuff.' His voice was husky. 'Still, if you want to try ...'

She laughed. 'I'll survive without it. Check in, Superman. Let's talk business. I'm hungry.'

By now the fat Negro in charge of the office had come to know Vin. He had never seen Judy as she always remained in the car while Vin checked in. Seeing Vin come into the office, the Negro glanced through the window, saw the Jaguar and then grinned at Vin.

'Evening, sir.' He pushed the register towards Vin. 'Nice seeing you again. I've got your usual cabin free.'

'Fine.' Vin signed the register as Steve Hamish. 'We won't be long, Jerry. Just a couple of hours.'

'You stay as long or as short as you like, Mr Hamish.'

Vin gave him a five dollar bill, then taking the key the Negro offered him, he returned to the Jaguar.

'All set ... the usual,' he said, opening the car door.

They walked together to the cabin and as soon as they were inside, Vin shot the bolt.

157

Judy wandered over to the bed and sat on it.

'So you sent the girl to find the stamps,' she said. 'Did she find them?'

Vin went to the refrigerator. He felt in need of a drink. 'Scotch?'

'Yes ... did she find them?'

He poured the Scotch into two glasses, then turned.

'You give and then I'll give,' he said and carried the drink over to her. 'What's the name of the buyer?' He offered the glass and stood over her. 'You tell me that and I'll tell you if she found the stamps.'

She took the glass and smiled up at him.

'When you have the stamps and when you have shown them to me I'll tell you the name of the buyer. We've gone over this routine before ... remember? But in case you are suffering from amnesia, I take the stamps to the buyer, collect the money and pay you off ... remember? We have also gone over that routine before.'

Vin took a long pull at his glass. So he would have to take action, he thought. Well, okay, she couldn't say she hadn't asked for it. He would have to get her off her guard, then slam a punch at her jaw. He mustn't make a mistake. He would have to knock her cold with the first punch or else the bitch would start yelling her head off.

'She knows where he keeps them,' he said, moving away from the bed. He sat down in a nearby chair. 'I can get them. I'll try tomorrow night.'

'How did she do it?'

He shrugged.

'Don't worry about that ... she did it and I'll get them tomorrow night.'

She sipped her drink, regarding him over the rim of the glass.

'Do you read gangster stories, Superman?'

He gaped at her. She was always asking unexpected questions that threw him.

'No ... I watch TV. I don't read books.'

'I read a gangster book the other night.' she said. 'It was about a brainless moron who was hired to kill people. Guess how he killed them?'

Vin put his glass down on the occasional table. Her steady, probing stare brought him out into a sweat.

'Who the hell cares? Let's talk business.'

'I thought you might have read the book. It's called, *Dollars are for Dames.*'

'I don't read books.'

'That's right ... you told me. Well, this moron carried a dog lead around with him. He strangled people with it.'

Suddenly Vin could smell his own sweat. A quick jump across to her, his fingers on her throat to throttle back her scream, then a slam on the jaw. Once he had got her gagged and bound, he would teach her to act tricky with him. He braced himself. One quick jump. He could hear yells and gunfire from the TV in the next cabin. Even if she did yell before he could shut her mouth, no one would pay any attention.

'Are you married, Superman?' Judy asked, nursing her drink.

This question so surprised Vin's slow working mind that he paused as he prepared himself for his spring forward.

'Married?' He gaped at her. 'No ... why the hell do you keep asking stupid questions?'

'Are you sure you haven't a jealous wife?' Her eyes were mocking now.

'What's with it?' He got to his feet and began to move casually towards her. 'I haven't a goddamn wife.' Three more steps and he would be within range.

'Then why are these two men following us?' Judy asked. 'I thought they were private dicks after divorce evidence.'

Vin felt as if he had walked into a wall. A wave of cold blood rushed up his spine. It was only at this moment that he remembered Elliot's warning to watch out that he wasn't followed. He remembered that Joey and Cindy had said they had been tailed.

'Following us?' His voice was strangled. 'What do you mean?'

His expression of fear, vicious frustration and alarm seemed to amuse her. She giggled.

'They followed us last night and they followed us tonight.' She put her head on one side and looked cute. 'Didn't you spot them, Superman?'

'Why didn't you tell me?' he snarled.

'I like having them around.' She smiled at him. 'They give me a feeling of security.'

Vin drew in a slow breath. She was wise to him! The shock hit him and he found his legs were unsteady. He sat down abruptly. What an escape! Suppose he had knocked her off! Imagine carting her body from the cabin to the Jag and as he was putting her body in the boot, these two punks had descended on him. The thought made sweat run down his face. What an escape!

'Have they upset your plans?' she asked. 'How sad! Did you really think I'm so dopey as to come here without protection? You and your dog lead!' She put her glass down and throwing back her head, she began to laugh.

Vin sat like a stricken bull. Finally he could stand the sound of her laughter no longer.

'Shut up, you goddamn bitch!' he bellowed.

She stopped laughing and taking a handkerchief from her bag, she mopped her eyes.

'Superman! You're the funniest thing alive. I knew you were stupid, but I didn't believe you could be such a brainless moron as you are.'

Vin half started from his chair, but, with an effort, he controlled the urge to grab her by her throat and strangle her.

'Cut it out!' he snarled. 'You and me are partners. I know where the stamps are and you know where the buyer is. We both want the money. Do we go ahead with this or don't we?' She regarded him and her face became as hard as stone.

'Yes ... we go ahead.' Her voice now had a cutting edge that startled Vin. 'Now listen to me, you stinking creep. You planned to force me to give you the name of the buyer and then you planned to murder me and take all the money for yourself. You're so obvious an idiot child could read the mess you call your mind! Make no mistake about this: you're going to get the stamps and you're going to give them to me! Don't imagine, you stupid clown, you can get them and take off. I'll know if they go and I'll give the police a description of you and they'll pick you up so fast you won't know what's hit you. From now on, Superduper, you're going to do what I tell you to do. There'll be no more cosy motels. When we meet, we meet with people around us so get the idea out of your moronic head that you'll ever get a chance of murdering me. Understand?'

Vin eyed her. The expression in her hard, cold eyes warned him to play it cool. This bitch was dangerous. If she put the cops on him ... but dare she? She would get involved herself.

'My father wouldn't bring a charge against me, Superduper,' Judy said. 'I know what you're thinking. Just

161

step out of turn and you'll have the fuzz crawling over you like fleas on a dog.'

Vin wiped the sweat off his face. He realized with sick frustration she was too goddamn smart for him to cope with.

'Okay,' he said. 'I'll get the stamps and then we'll do a deal.'

'It's going to be a different kind of deal, little man,' Judy said. 'You will now get a hundred thousand and I'm having the rest. Now get out! I'll take a taxi home. When you have the stamps, telephone me and we'll meet at the Plaza Beach. If the stamps go and I don't hear from you, the fuzz will be after you. That's a promise ... now, get out!'

Vin hesitated. This could be his last chance to be alone with her. Suppose she was bluffing? Suppose they hadn't been tailed? Dare he take the risk? His fingers itched to fasten on her throat.

Judy faced him, her eyes contemptuous.

'Just try it, you stinker, and see where it gets you!' she said in a fierce whisper. 'Get out!'

With a feeling of frustrated defeat and fury, Vin turned and stamped out of the cabin.

*   *   *

Soon after Vin had gone to meet Judy, for no reason at all Elliot's nonexistent foot began to ache. This pain always put Elliot in a bad mood and saying curtly he wanted to read, he went to his room, leaving Cindy and Joey to settle to television.

Lying on his bed, Elliot again considered his future. He realized that Cindy had made an unexpected difference to his outlook. He now had the stamps. He was sure Vin planned to double cross them all ... so why not double cross Vin? Why not take the stamps to Kendrick, try to get

162

the price upped or if Kendrick wouldn't play to accept the two hundred thousand dollars and with Cindy and Joey, take off, leaving Vin to whistle for his share?

But Elliot realized after some thought that it wasn't in him to double cross anyone. He knew Cindy wouldn't approve and if he did it he knew for the rest of his days he would have put himself on the same level as Vin and that was unthinkable.

Vin had said he would get the name of the buyer from the Larrimore girl. After all, five hundred thousand was a lot better than two hundred thousand. Elliot found he had no qualms about double crossing Kendrick. After all, Kendrick had swindled him in the past. No, he had no qualms about Kendrick.

He was still thinking, turning over in his mind whether, once he got the money, to join up with Cindy and Joey or whether to take off and have a bell of a splurge and then take sleeping pills, when he heard Vin come into the bungalow.

He heard him say: 'Where's Elliot? Okay ... you keep out of this! I've got to talk to him and that doesn't include you two!'

From the sound of Vin's voice, Elliot guessed he was in a vicious rage. He swung his legs off the bed and sat up.

Vin came into the small room, kicked the door shut and stood glaring at Elliot.

'She didn't play?' Elliot asked quietly.

During the drive back to the bungalow, Vin had thought until his brain had creaked. He realized that Judy had outsmarted him. He had a feeling that once she got the stamps she would gyp him out of this hundred thousand she was offering and there would be nothing he could do about it. She had said her father wouldn't bring a charge against her but that didn't mean the old punk wouldn't bring a charge against him! With frustrated fury he finally accepted the bitter fact that he hadn't the brains to cope with a situation like this. If anyone could cope with it it was this punk movie star and Vin decided he would have to put his cards – not all of them – on the table and be willing to accept part of the take and not all of it.

'No ... the bitch!' Vin clenched and unclenched his hands. 'She won't tell me who the buyer is until I give her the stamps and she insists on dealing with the buyer herself!'

Elliot began to rub his tin foot while he regarded Vin.

'Then you owe me a thousand dollars,' he said.

Vin took the roll from his pocket and threw it on the bed. He watched Elliot count the money and transfer it to his pocket.

'Don't worry about her,' Elliot said. 'We'll go for the lower figure. I've got the stamps.'

Vin stood motionless, a glazed look coming into his eyes.

'You've got them?' he said hoarsely. 'What the hell are you saying?'

'Cindy got them.'

Vin sat abruptly on a chair.

'You mean when she saw Larrimore, she got at the stamps?'

'That's right.'

Vin began to sweat.

'When Larrimore misses them we'll have a load of fuzz here!'

Elliot shook his head. 'For some reason I don't understand, Larrimore was warned two months ago that he would be prosecuted if he had the stamps and kept them. He can't complain to the police now unless he wants to risk a prosecution by the CIA.'

'The ... who?'

'The CIA.'

Vin gaped at him.

'You mean the Government jerks who spy and play general hell?'

Elliot nodded.

'But what have they to do with the stamps?'

'I'm trying to figure that one out myself.'

Vin's mind was in a whirl. 'Where are the stamps?'

'In a safe deposit. I'll see Kendrick tomorrow. Maybe I can squeeze more money out of him. Forget Judy. If we are lucky we could get another fifty thousand out of Kendrick. As you didn't get the stamps, your share goes down to fifty thousand and as Cindy got them, her share goes up to a hundred.'

Vin drew in a snorting breath. He saw now that he would have to put his final card on the table. He hesitated for a long moment, but if Elliot sold the stamps for a mere two hundred and fifty, Vin knew he would have nightmares for the rest of his days.

'Do you know how much these goddamn stamps are worth?' he demanded, sitting forward and glaring at Elliot. 'Do you?'

'Yes. That bitch told me. Larrimore was offered a million for them and you are talking of selling them for two hundred and fifty!'

For a moment Elliot stared at Vin, then he shook his head.

'She was conning you. No stamps are worth that kind of money.'

'That letter I told you she had seen. She didn't know I was interested in the stamps when she told me,' Vin said feverishly. 'That's what they're worth! A million! That's why she won't play. She wants all that money for herself!'

Elliot felt a prickle run up his spine. Could it be possible? he asked himself. If he could lay his hands on

165

that amount of money he could clear his debts and make a new start. A million!

'I can't believe it!'

'I'm telling you,' Vin said violently, 'and I'll tell you something else ... this bitch told me she'd give the cops a description of me if she found the stamps missing. You hear? As soon as her goddamn father tells her Cindy has taken the stamps, we'll have the fuzz in our laps!'

Elliot waved this away.

'She'll never know they are missing,' he said. 'If Larrimore can't tell the police they have gone is it likely he would tell her who he dislikes?'

Vin hadn't thought of this. He relaxed a little.

'You can forget her,' Elliot went on. 'There must be some other way to find out who this buyer is without getting involved with her. Kendrick knows. Larrimore knows. Neither of them would tell us. Who else would know?'

Vin shuffled uneasily.

'Search me, and I'll tell you something else ... I was followed last night and tonight. I didn't spot them but Judy did.' Elliot stiffened.

'If she did ... why didn't you?'

'I had things on my mind,' Vin said sullenly. 'I forgot to check.'

'Could she have been conning you?'

Vin's eyes narrowed. He hadn't thought of that. By spinning a yarn that they were being watched she had saved her goddamn neck. Yes ... she could have been smart enough to have conned him.

'Maybe ... I don't know. Someone followed Joey and Cindy.'

Elliot got to his feet. 'This bothers me. Let's check and find out.' He left his room and went into the living-room. Vin, scowling, joined him.

'Joey ... I want to talk to you,' Elliot said.

Reluctantly, Joey turned off the TV set and regarded Elliot inquiringly.

'Vin thinks he was followed tonight. I want to be sure. He's going to take a walk down town. Give him a start, then go after him. See if you can spot the tailer.' He turned to Vin. 'Go to the end of the road and keep along Beechwood Drive until you come to the drug store. Buy some cigarettes and then come back ... take your time.'

'What's the matter with taking the car?' asked Vin who hated walking.

'Do what I say!' Elliot snapped.

Shrugging, Vin left the bungalow and after giving him a three minute start, Joey went after him.

'What is it, Don?' Cindy asked anxiously. 'Do you really think someone's following us?'

'If there is someone, Joey should spot him.' Elliot turned to the door. 'Go to bed. I've got thinking to do.'

'I'll wait for dad to get back.'

'Cindy!' The snap in Elliot's voice startled her. 'Go to bed and stay in your room no matter what you hear. Do you understand?'

'What's going to happen?'

'For God's sake, don't be a nuisance! Go to bed!'

With a hurt expression on her face, Cindy left the room. Elliot grimaced, then sat down and waited for Vin and Joey to return.

Half an hour later, Vin came in.

'Anything?'

'Not a damn thing! No one followed me,' Vin said sourly. 'A waste of time.'

'Let's wait for Joey.'

Twenty minutes later Joey came in and quietly shut the door.

'He was followed and so was I,' he said. 'One of them is in the back garden right now.'

'Did you see him?' Elliot asked, getting to his feet.

'Yes … he's behind the big shrub at the end of the garden. There's no place else for him to hide. The other one is in a car at the end of the road.'

'Okay, Joey … you've done a swell job. Now, go to bed.'

'Cindy in bed?'

'Yes.'

Joey looked at Vin, hesitated, then moved to the door.

'Well, then … good night.'

When he had gone, Elliot said softly, 'Let's go get him. Maybe we can persuade him to tell us who he is working for.'

Vin's face lit up with a wolfish grin.

'If it's to be told, he'll tell. How do we take him?'

'Let's look.'

The two men went into the dark kitchen and Elliot closed the door. They went to the window and looked out on to the back garden. Although there was a big moon the tall trees surrounding the garden made it dark, but they could make out the outline of the big flowering shrub at the bottom of the garden.

'I'll crawl down there and flush him out,' Elliot said. 'When you hear me call, come fast.'

Vin nodded. This was the kind of action he liked. He was impressed by the way Elliot slid out through the back door and disappeared into the darkness. He waited, then hearing a sudden commotion, he charged down the lawn and blundered on Elliot, kneeling over a limp body.

'Okay,' Elliot said, standing up. 'I've fixed him. He was half asleep. He'll be out for ten minutes or so. Help me carry him in.'

Together, they carried the unconscious man into the kitchen, down a short passage and into the living-room.

'Lock the door,' Elliot said as they dumped the man on the settee.

Vin locked the door and joined Elliot to look down at the man on the settee. He wasn't much to look at: below average height, small boned, sandy haired, round, boyish face and at a guess, Elliot thought he couldn't be more than twenty years of age.

'Not much of a punk, is he?' Vin said. 'What did you do … knock him on the nut?'

'Chop at the back of his neck,' Elliot said. 'He'll be all right in a few minutes.'

The name of the man lying on the settee was Jim Folls. He had joined Lessing's investigators as a learner two months ago. With all Lessing's top investigators concentrating on Larrimore's house, Nisson had thought it safe to leave Folls to keep an eye on Elliot's bungalow. He had told him to do nothing but sit behind the shrub and leave it to Ross, parked in a car at the end of the road, to take care of anything that might happen. Folls' job was to alert Ross by his transceiver if anyone left the bungalow. But Folls had taken a correspondence course in detective work and was keen. When he saw Vin leave the bungalow he not only alerted Ross, but followed Vin just in case Ross made a box up of it. He hadn't any opinion of Ross' talents. By doing so he had given himself away to Joey who spotted him sneaking after Vin.

'He's coming to the surface now,' Elliot said. 'We'll scare the crap out of him. He doesn't look as if he has any resistance.'

'I'll handle him,' Vin said viciously. 'This is right up my alley.'

Folls stirred, moaned, blinked and then half sat up. When he found himself staring into Vin's hard, vicious face, he shrank back, catching his breath in horror.

Vin caught hold of Folls' shirt front, lifted him slightly and shook him.

'Okay, rat ... what were you doing out there?' he snarled.

Folls' mind spun like a top. When in a tight corner, his correspondence course had told him, act cool, bluff and show no sign of fear.

Strictly against this advice, Folls quaked with fear, couldn't get his brain to work and just gazed with horror at the menacing figure bending over him.

'Don't hurt me ...' he finally managed to splutter.

'Hurt you?' Vin snarled. 'I'm going to tear your goddamn arm off and beat you to death with it!'

'Strictly B movie dialogue,' Elliot said disapprovingly. 'We don't have to do that. What we can do is to put burning cigarettes on his naked feet. It's an old Japanese custom and it works fine.'

Folls looked as if he were going to faint. Vin let go of him and stepped back. Folls huddled on the settee, staring up at the two men, quivering and wishing he had remained a grocer's assistant and hadn't been crazy enough to volunteer to be one of Lessing's investigators.

'Yeah,' Vin said. 'I dig that. Let's do it.' He grabbed hold of one of Polls' feet and dragged off his shoe and sock.

Into Folls' panic stricken mind came the heading of Chapter Six of his correspondence course: *if subject to torture, remember your loyalty to your boss always comes first. A top class investigator never talks.*

He fervently wished the writer of this course was now in his position. He was ready to bet the creep would sing like a canary.

'I'll talk,' he said breathlessly. 'I'll tell you anything you want to know!'

Vin sneered. 'Yeah? Well, let's try a little burning first.' He took a cigarette from his pack and lit it.

'Hold it,' Elliot said. 'I'll talk to him.'

'Just let me mash this on his foot,' Vin said. 'It'll loosen him up.'

'Keep smoking. You can have a go at him if he doesn't come clean. There's no point in having to carry this punk out of here. Once you start on him he won't be able to walk for weeks.'

Folls shuddered.

'Why are you tailing us?' Elliot demanded.

Folls had been warned by Nisson that if the suspects got an idea that they were being watched not only would he lose his job but Nisson would also lose his, but Folls was too scared by now to think up a convincing lie and seeing Vin was itching to burn him, he said in a quavering voice, 'I was only acting on instructions.'

'Who are you working for?'

'The Lessing Agency.'

Elliot knew of the agency which was the best and the most expensive in the City.

'What are your instructions?'

'Just to watch you all ... see where you go ... what you do and make reports.'

'Why?'

Folls licked his dry lips and hesitated.

171

'Let me just mash this cigarette on his foot,' Vin said. 'Just once. He needs loosening up,' and he started forward.

Folls' eyes popped wide open.

'No ... no! They think you're going to break into Mr Larrimore's house. They plan to catch you as you come out.'

'Who are they?' Elliot asked.

'Mr Lessing and his investigators.'

'How many of them are on the job?'

'Six now ... before they found where you are living, they had about thirty men looking for you.'

Elliot and Vin exchanged looks.

'Are you anything to do with the CIA?' Elliot asked.

'The CIA? No, sir. I just work for Mr Lessing.'

'Who hired Lessing to watch us?'

'I don't know.' Then seeing Vin's menacing move forward, he repeated in a shriller voice, 'I swear I don't know!'

Elliot decided he was telling the truth. Why should a punk like this be told the names of Lessing's clients? 'Thirty men looking for you,' Folls had said. At Lessing's rates an operation on this scale would cost a lot of money.

'Who's Lessing's most important client? You must know that,' Elliot said.

'I don't know. We're never told anything about anyone who hires us. I'd tell you if I knew.'

With an impatient snort, Vin flicked hot ash on Folls' bare foot. Folls reared up as if he had been touched by a red hot iron.

'Don't do it!' His voice cracked. 'I've heard them talking about someone, but he mightn't even be a client. I just heard a name.'

'What name?' Elliot asked.

'I heard Nisson and Ross talking. They talked about a man called Herman Radnitz who lives at the Belvedere Hotel.'

Radnitz!

Elliot stiffened. His mind went back to a big cocktail party thrown by the Vice-President of MGM when he was on vacation in Paradise City. Elliot, along with four hundred other celebrities, had been invited. The one man who had made an impression on him among all the rich and the famous had been a toadlike, fat financier who someone had told him was the most important wheeler dealer in the world. His name had stuck: Herman Radnitz. 'A man who has dealings with the Soviet Union,' his informer had told him. 'Come to that, he has dealings with every foreign government and is on first name terms with the President.'

Concealing his excitement, Elliot asked, 'Who are Nisson and Ross?'

'They lead the investigation ... Ross is out there in the car.' Vin was listening to all this with growing impatience. 'Let's set about this creep. He's got more up his jersey than he's spilling.'

Elliot was satisfied. He shook his head. 'Get your sock and shoe on,' he said to Folls. 'I could turn you over to the police, but I'm not going to. You keep your mouth shut and I'll keep mine shut. Go ahead and watch us. We're doing nothing wrong and we have no intention of breaking into Larrimore's house. That's someone's pipe dream. You start something and I'll start something. Okay?'

'Are you letting this creep go?' Vin asked, gaping at Elliot.

'That's right. Let him watch us. What have we to worry about?' Elliot turned slightly so Folls couldn't see and winked at Vin.

Vin, baffled, moved to the door and unlocked it.

'Get the hell out of here!' he snarled at Folls.

Scared witless, Folls bolted down the passage and out into the garden.

Elliot regarded Vin.

'I think he gave it away,' he said. 'Herman Radnitz. There's no one in this City except him who could offer a million for those Russian stamps. He has dealings, with Russia. He fits, but now I want to find out why he wants these stamps so badly.'

'Who cares as long as he pays out?'

'He's big time and dangerous. He could put you on the ball of his thumb and make a smear of you on a wall.'

'Oh, yeah?' Vin sneered. 'Rich punks don't scare me.'

'There are times, Vin, when I despair of you.' Elliot moved to the door. 'I'm going to bed.'

'Hey, wait a minute! Are you seeing this guy tomorrow?'

'No. I have to be sure he really is the one who wants the stamps. At the moment, I'm guessing. Then I'll have to think of a way to handle the deal.'

'What's so tough about it?' Vin demanded impatiently. 'You go to him, tell him you have the stamps, you want a million, get the money and give him the stamps. What's wrong with that? If you don't want to handle it, I'll handle it!'

'As I said, there are times when I despair of you,' Elliot said and left the room.

The following morning, Elliot joined Joey and Cindy for breakfast. Vin was still in bed. Both Joey and Cindy were intensely curious about what had happened the previous night and Elliot told them.

'I feel pretty certain Radnitz is our man,' he concluded, 'but before I approach him I must find out just why the CIA are interested in these stamps. To get the CIA after us would be serious.' He looked over at Cindy. 'Can you remember who signed the circular letter you found with the stamps?'

'Lee Humphrey,' Cindy told him. 'It was a rubber stamp signature.'

'Right. You and I are going to Miami this morning. We'll take the Alfa. If you drive, the chances are no one will spot me.'

'Why Miami, Don?'

'I'm calling Washington and it could be traced,' Elliot said. 'When dealing with the CIA you can't be too careful. I'll call from a hotel.'

All this worried Joey, but he said nothing. At least, he told himself, Elliot seemed to know what be was doing.

Soon after 10.00, Elliot and Cindy left the bungalow. Joey had been told not to tell Vin where they were going. It wasn't until 10.30 that Vin made his appearance.

Vin had spent most of the night thinking. If Elliot was to be believed, he, Vin, now knew the name of the buyer and where to contact him. He also knew the stamps were in a safe deposit box in a bank. He was sure both Cindy and Joey knew in which bank.

He came into the living-room to find Joey preparing to go out. He paused, looking suspiciously at him.

'Where are you going?'

'To get lunch.' Joey was a little fearful of Vin. Gone were the days when he could relax with him. 'Anything I can get you?'

'Where are the other two?'

'They've gone out. Do you fancy a steak for lunch?'

'Gone out?' Vin's eyes narrowed. 'Where have they gone?'

'Taking a day off on the beach,' Joey said, and started towards the door.

Vin caught hold of his arm and swung him around. The vicious expression on his face scared Joey.

'Don't feed me that crap!' he snarled. 'Where have they gone?'

'They said to the beach and they wouldn't be back for lunch,' Joey said feebly. His lying wouldn't have convinced a child.

Vin pointed to a chair. 'Sit down!'

'Not now, Vin. I've got to buy the lunch,' Joey said desperately. 'I'm late as it is.'

'Sit down!' Vin repeated and there was a look in his eyes that turned Joey's legs weak. He sat down.

'Where are the stamps, Joey?' Joey licked his dry lips.

'I don't know. Don handled them. He didn't tell me.'

'You'd better know, Joey,' Vin said viciously. 'Where are they?'

'All I know is they're in a bank,' Joey said, flinching at the expression on Vin's face.

'What bank?'

'He didn't tell me.'

'Listen, you stupid old creep, Elliot didn't take the stamps to the bank. He's too scared to show his face on main street. Either you or Cindy took them,' Vin snarled. 'You think I'm a dope? Now, listen, I want those stamps and I'm going to have them. I'm going to show you something.' He took from his pocket a small blue bottle with a rubber stopper. 'Know what this is?'

Joey eyed the bottle the way a snake eyes a mongoose. 'No ...'

'I'll tell you,' Vin said. 'It's sulphuric acid.' Joey wasn't to know the bottle contained harmless eye-drops. He stared at the bottle, his eyes growing round. 'You're going to give me those stamps,' Vin went on. 'You're going to the bank right away and you're going to bring them back here. I've had all I'm going to take from you three jerks. I want the stamps or Cindy will lose her looks. Don't kid yourself, Joey. Neither you nor Elliot can protect her. Okay, maybe for a few days, but you can't live with her all the time and sooner or later I'll catch up with her. One flick of my wrist and she gets this little lot in her face. Have you ever seen acid burns?'

Joey felt a cold sickness creep over him. He stared at Vin, his heart beating so fast he felt suffocated.

'I'm not bluffing, Joey. Get the stamps. I won't tell you a second time.'

'You – you wouldn't do that to Cindy,' Joey said huskily.

'Get the stamps. I'll wait here. I'll give you two hours. If in two hours you're not back, I'm leaving, but I'll be around. I promise you one thing, if you don't bring the stamps back, Cindy gets it within a week or so. That's a promise! Now, get off!'

Suddenly Joey felt a wave of relief run through him. When Vin had the stamps, he would leave the bungalow and they would be rid of him. Not only rid of him, but the operation would be abortive. He didn't want all this money. He had never wanted to take such a risk. He would explain to Cindy just why he had handed over the stamps and she would understand. With any luck, they would get rid of Elliot too and would then be able to settle down once again to their old life. It was a good life, Joey told himself. Maybe in a few years time, Cindy would find a decent man and they would get married. All right ... she had said she was in love with Elliot, but once Elliot was off the scene, she would forget him.

'I'm going,' Joey said. 'I'll get the stamps. You just wait here.'

With an almost jaunty step, he left the bungalow.

Through the window, Vin watched him go. Joey's sudden change of attitude baffled him.

'The old goat's nutty,' he thought. 'Goddamn it! He looks almost happy!'

Shrugging, he crossed the room and picked up the telephone book. He found the number of the Belvedere hotel and dialled it.

'Put me through to Mr Radnitz,' he said when the receptionist came on the line.

There was a delay, then Holtz, who took all incoming calls, said, 'Mr Herman Radnitz's secretary.'

'Give me Mr Radnitz,' Vin said.

'Who is calling?'

'Never mind. I've got business with him.'

'Please state your business in writing,' Holtz said and hung up.

For a long moment, his face red with fury, Vin stared at the telephone, then he dialled the hotel again.

Again Holtz came on the line.

'I want to talk to Radnitz!' Vin snarled. 'Tell him it's to do with stamps.'

At the other end Holtz stiffened to attention.

'Your name?'

'Get stuffed, you goddamn dummy!' Vin bawled. 'Tell him!'

'Hold on.' Getting to his feet, Holtz went quickly out on to the terrace.

Radnitz was having a late cup of coffee.

'There's a man on the line who wants to talk to you, sir,' Holtz said. 'He won't give his name but he says it is to do with stamps.'

Radnitz put down his cup.

'Put him through and trace the call,' he said.

A moment later, Vin heard a guttural voice say, 'This is Radnitz. Who are you?'

'Never mind.' Vin was sweating with excitement. A Big Shot like Radnitz wouldn't have come on the line unless he was the guy who wanted the stamps. This meant Elliot had guessed right. 'Are you interested in eight Russian stamps?'

There was a pause, then Radnitz said, 'Yes, I am interested.'

Vin paused. He wasn't sure how to play this.

'I said I was interested,' Radnitz said sharply as he heard nothing but a quiet humming over the line. 'Have you got them?'

'I've got them.' Vin wiped the sweat from his face. 'What are they worth to you?'

'We are talking over an open line,' Radnitz said smoothly. 'I suggest you come and see me. Come right away.'

Vin suddenly relaxed. So this rich, powerful punk was that eager, he thought.

'I'll call back. I'm busy right now. Maybe I can fit you in sometime tonight,' he said and he hung up.

Leaning on the table, staring at the telephone, he felt a surge of power. A million dollars! Maybe he could squeeze a million and a half out of this punk! So he called the President by his first name! So he was the biggest wheeler dealer in the world! Well, Vin thought, I'll show him! If he wants these stamps so goddamn bad, then he'll sweat for them.

Holtz came across the terrace to where Radnitz was sitting, staring out to sea.

'The call was from the Seagull bungalow, sir.'

'It would be this man Pinna?'

'Yes.'

'Have you Lessing's report for this morning?'

'Yes, sir. Elliot and Miss Luck left the bungalow at 10.00. They are being followed. Luck left at 10.45. He is also being followed.'

Radnitz nodded. 'Keep me informed,' he said and waved Holtz away.

* * *

At the Excelsior hotel, Elliot shut himself in an air conditioned telephone booth and waited for his connection to CIA headquarters, Washington.

Through the glass panel he could see Cindy sitting across the lounge, looking anxiously at him. He waved to her as he was connected. He asked to speak to Mr Lee Humphrey. He went through the usual rigmarole of talking to an undersecretary, then to a secretary, then finally Humphrey came on the line himself.

'Mr Humphrey, I wish to remain anonymous,' Elliot said. 'I understand your organization is interested in eight Russian stamps.'

There was no hesitation in Humphrey's booming voice as he said, 'That is correct. If you have any information regarding these stamps, it is your duty to the State to give that information right here and now.'

Elliot grimaced.

'My duty to the State? Would you expand on that?'

'The State wants these stamps. Every philatelist in the country has been notified to this effect. There is a penalty of three years' imprisonment and a thirty thousand dollar fine if anyone holding these stamps does not send them immediately to me.'

'Can you tell me, Mr Humphrey, just why these stamps are so important to the State?'

'I can't tell you that. Have you the stamps?'

'It would make a difference if I knew,' Elliot said. 'If you will be frank with me and tell me just why these stamps are so important I will answer your question.'

'I can't tell you over an open line. If you have these stamps or know where they are or have any information it is your duty to go to the nearest CIA office and either deliver the stamps or give information.'

'You keep talking about duty, Mr Humphrey. I've been offered a million dollars for these stamps. Is the State making an offer?'

'That we can discuss. So you have them?'

'I'll call you back later,' Elliot said, aware that he had talked long enough on this telephone. He hung up. Taking out his handkerchief, he carefully wiped the receiver, then the door handle of the booth. Satisfied he had got rid of any fingerprints, he walked over to where Cindy was sitting.

She could see by the expression on his face he was worried.

'What is it, Don?'

He told her of the conversation he had had with Humphrey and as she listened, her eyes grew round.

'Duty to the State?' She put her hand on his. 'What does that mean?'

'The CIA aren't dramatic,' Elliot said. 'It seems to me we'll have to give them the stamps. The last thing we want is to get the CIA after us.'

'Let's go home, get the stamps and send them,' Cindy said. 'What do you think they can mean ... duty to the State?'

Elliot gave her a little nudge as two big men, quietly dressed, came swiftly into the hotel lounge. One of them went to the girl who was in control of the switchboard, spoke to her, then went to the booth where Elliot had made his call.

'The CIA,' Elliot said. 'Just take it easy. I want to see what they do.'

One of the men was closely dusting the receiver for fingerprints while the other went to the hall porter and began to question him.

'Okay, Cindy, let's go.' Elliot got casually to his feet.

The hotel lobby was swarming with tourists and by walking slowly, pushing their way through the crowd, they attracted no attention.

'I've got to talk to Humphrey again,' Elliot said. 'We'll drive to Dayton Beach.'

They got into the Alfa Romeo and Elliot headed north. Cindy looked anxiously at him as he drove. There was a bitter expression on his face now and it frightened her.

'Don ... let's go back,' she said. 'It doesn't matter. We can get by. We don't have to have this money. If you'll stay with dad and me ...'

'Skip it,' Elliot said curtly. 'I told you how it was going to be, Cindy. There's something fatal about me. We've met ... we've liked each other ... we've had a good time together, that's as far as it's going to go. Just take it easy ... I want to think.'

Cindy relapsed into silence: her hands into fists, gripped between her knees.

As Elliot drove up the broad highway, his mind wrestled with the problem. For some important reason, these stamps were at priority. The CIA wouldn't have said this unless it was true. 'Your duty to the State.' Against that there was Radnitz offering a million. Radnitz had dealings with the Soviet Union. This must mean that the Russians were as anxious to get the stamps as were the CIA. If he gave the stamps to Humphrey in the hope he would be paid a reward, he was certain Humphrey would want to know from whom he had got the stamps and this would involve Larrimore. That was, to Elliot, unthinkable. The only way was to mail the stamps to Humphrey and kiss the million goodbye.

'The money doesn't matter,' Cindy had said, and he could believe that. She and Joey had lived for years on a shoestring, stealing, living simply and they could go back to their old way of life. Vin didn't matter. He would always look after himself.

Elliot whipped the Alfa past a Cadillac as he turned his thoughts to himself. This was the end of the road, he thought. Well, what did it matter? He had had fun for eight or nine days: something he couldn't remember having had for a long, long time. It was still a good movie script. He had outfoxed Vin without the aid of the scriptwriters. He would talk again to Humphrey and tell him that the stamps were on their way. He would drive Cindy back to Paradise City. Tell Vin the operation was abortive. He was confident he could take care of Vin if Vin turned ugly. Then, he would walk out, get in the Alfa and drive to Hollywood. Sleeping pills would take care of the rest of the story. His non-existent foot began to ache. He, would be better off, he thought, with no future. He remembered what he had said to Cindy: 'You're dead without money'. He glanced at her. She was sitting motionless, looking through the windshield, her lips parted, her face a mask of misery. For a little while, he thought, she would suffer, but she was young. In a year or so, he would be just a romantic memory. He reached out and patted her hand.

'It'll work out, Cindy,' he said. 'It always does.'

She didn't look at him, but she moved her hand and gripped his.

Later, he pulled up outside the Beach hotel at Dayton Beach.

'Wait here, Cindy,' he said. 'I won't be long.'

During the drive they had scarcely spoken and Cindy was in despair. She felt now she had lost this man who meant so much to her. A barrier had grown up between them and she was fearful of what he intended to do.

Again inside an air conditioned telephone booth, Elliot called Humphrey.

'Mr Humphrey,' Elliot said as soon as he was connected, 'you can call off your men. Don't try to find me. I'm sending you the stamps by registered mail. You will have them the day after tomorrow. The only condition is you won't try to find me. If you act smart and I get picked up, I assure you you will never get the stamps. Okay?'

'If the stamps don't arrive on my desk by the day after tomorrow,' Humphrey said, his voice curt, 'we'll come after you. I have a tape recording of your voice. You'll be in the middle of the biggest man hunt this country has ever staged. I'll give you until the day after tomorrow and then, if you haven't delivered, you're in trouble.'

This could be a James Bond movie script, Elliot thought. Well, the stamps would arrive and he wouldn't be in that kind of trouble.

184

'Let's hope we don't have a mail strike,' he said, and hung up.

*   *   *

As soon as Vin had hung up on his conversation with Radnitz, he went to his bedroom and packed his things. He was so elated with the thought that within a very short time he would be worth a million dollars he was almost tempted to leave all his old clothes, that soon he could buy himself a complete new wardrobe. Once the bag was packed, he looked around the room, made sure he had left nothing, then dropping his .38 automatic into his hip pocket, he carried the bag into the living-room.

Lighting a cigarette, he went to the window. It would take Joey a good hour to get down town, collect the stamps and return. Well, that was all right with Vin. He could wait ... just so long as Joey did come back. Vin told himself that Joey was so spineless he would get the stamps. He grinned to himself as he thought of how he had scared the crap out of Joey with a bottle of eye drops.

While he stood by the window, he thought of Radnitz. He could be tricky. Suppose he tried a double cross? A million was a hell of a lot of money. Radnitz wouldn't give him that sum in cash.

Vin rubbed his jaw while he thought. How to work this?

After a while and having made his brain creak, he decided he and Radnitz would meet at Radnitz's bank. Before a bank witness, Vin would hand over the stamps in return for a certified cheque. That seemed to be the safe and only way to block a double cross. Radnitz would have to remain in the bank until the money had been transferred by Telex to Vin's New York bank. Satisfied that he had solved this problem, he continued to wait, his mind roving into the future. Man! What would he do with all this bread! He had always wanted a yacht. Okay, so he would buy a yacht. He would buy one of those big estates in Bermuda the pictures of which he had so often seen in the coloured glossies. He would fill the house with willing dollies. Man! Would he live it up! Then when he wanted a change he would get aboard his yacht with one special chick and take off into the sun. That was the way to live! Vin grinned. Two days ... then he would have the key that opened the door to a new, rich and exciting life!

He went on dreaming and waiting and the hands of his watch crept on. Vin didn't mind the wait. Who cared about waiting when a future so full of everything he wanted made coloured pictures in his mind?

Then he saw Joey coming up the path leading to the bungalow. Vin watched him. The jaunty, sprightly step and Joey's relaxed, almost happy expression baffled Vin. It was as if Joey was receiving a million dollars rather than losing them.

Vin went to the front door and jerked it open as Joey reached the steps.

'Did you get them?' Vin demanded, aware his voice was unsteady.

'I've got them,' Joey said and moving past Vin, he entered the living-room.

Vin went after him.

'Give!' He caught hold of Joey's arm, his face alight with greed and excitement.

Joey handed him an envelope. Vin snatched it and ripped it open. He took out a plastic envelope containing the eight stamps. He stared at them, his eyes gleaming.

'They don't look much, do they?'

Joey moved away from him, watching him.

'Lots of things don't look much,' he said quietly. 'You and me don't look much.'

Vin wasn't listening. He was gloating over the stamps. Finally, he put them in his pocket.

'Well, I'm on my way, Joey,' he said. 'Think of me rich! Man! Am I going to have a ball! Tell that dummy movie star from me to get stuffed! He thought he was smart. Tell him I'm smarter.' He went to pick up his bag while Joey watched him, saying nothing.

Vin paused and looked at him.

'You don't say much, do you, Joey?'

'What's there to say except I'm glad to see you go,' Joey said quietly. 'I hope you enjoy the money. Get going. Don could come back.'

'Yeah.' Vin started for the door, then again paused. 'So long, Joey. When next we meet if ever, I'll buy you a cigar.' He went quickly down the path to the waiting Jaguar.

Joey drew in a long, deep breath. So all that danger, risk, the threat of the cops was now finished, he thought. He would have to be careful how he explained it all to Cindy. Maybe if he explained it right, she would come to her senses, see that their way of life was the best way of life. He sat down limply in a chair, feeling suddenly depressed and very tired, but he knew – he was sure – that he had done the right thing. Who wanted all that money? You didn't have to have money to be happy, he assured himself. He closed his eyes and began to rehearse what he would tell Cindy.

*   *   *

'Being a writer, Mr Campbell,' Barney said as he finished what must have been his sixteenth beer, 'I don't have to tell you that every story has some loose ends. Now, this may

187

surprise you, but when I tell a story, I like to be neat: I like to tie up as many loose ends as I can.'

I said that was the hallmark of a good writer and it did him credit. He squinted at me suspiciously, not quite sure if I were conning him or not, but finally he decided I wasn't.

'Telling a story is like painting a picture,' he went on. 'You finally finish it and you sit back and look at it and you find there are still a few touches to make it perfect ... right?'

I nodded.

'Well, I'm going back to a corner of my picture that you might think I've neglected.' He scowled across the smoky, crowded bar and waved an urgent hand.

Sam shoved his way through the crowd, carrying the seventeenth beer and another vicious looking hamburger.

'Are you eating again?' I asked, not because I begrudged paying for this horrible abortion, but because I found it hard to believe any man, at one sitting, could work through three of these soggy messes, plus two dozen mouth exploding sausages.

'My midnight snack,' Barney said gravely. 'If I don't eat well, I don't sleep well. If there's one thing I like, apart from beer and talking, it's sleeping well.'

I said I understood.

'Well, now,' he said as he began to cut up the hamburger. 'I'm going to shift the scene just for a moment to the two hippies I told you about at the beginning of this story: Larry and Robo.' He chewed, then looked inquiringly at me. 'You remember them?'

I said I remembered them. They were the two Vin had run into when he had first met Judy Larrimore: the two Vin had fought with and had kicked around, busting Larry's nose.

Barney nodded approvingly.

'That's what I like about a professional,' he said. 'You keep track. You know something? I often tell punks a story and when I try to remind them of something I've told them, I find they are asleep.'

I said this was always a danger when telling people stories.

'Yeah.' He brooded darkly for a long moment, then went on: 'Larry and Robo: two stupid young punks who chased the chicks, smoked reefers, threw their weight around and generally made a nuisance of themselves. Not that there is anything unusual about that. They just followed the trend.' Barney swirled his beer around in his glass and shook his head. 'The trouble today, Mr Campbell is that it is too easy for young punks to earn money. When they've got it, they get into mischief. These two punks made money in a rattle snake factory. Their job was to skin the snakes while other punks put the snakes in cans. Doesn't sound much of a job, does it? But you'd be surprised. What with their union and the rest of it they made around a hundred and twenty dollars a week. That's nice money, isn't it?'

I said nothing would induce me to touch a rattle snake, dead or alive.

Barney pursed his lips.

'That's because of your artistic temperament, Mr Campbell. These punks aren't made like you.'

I said that was just as well for the canning factory.

'Yeah.' Barney ate more of the greasy hamburger. 'Well, these two were discharged from hospital at the identical moment Vin was getting into his Jaguar to call on Radnitz. Larry had got his nose fixed, but it was still sore and Robo had stopped passing blood. Vin's punch in his kidneys had upset his waterworks. They had only one thought in their minds and that was to get even with Vin. Not only had they had a bad time in hospital – the matron had made them

189

wash themselves – but they had lost money because when they stopped skinning snakes they stopped earning. So they were in a pretty mean mood. They had talked it over while in hospital and they had come to the conclusion that Vin was too tough for them to try to beat up. They weren't going to risk another spell in hospital. They decided to find out where he lived, wait until he had gone out, then break into his place and wreck it: smash everything and pour acid on all his clothes. They liked this idea because it was without risk to themselves and it would make Vin flip his lid. The first move them was to find out where he lived.

'Now the State hospital is within a stone's throw of the Belvedere hotel. As these two were coming down the steps of the hospital they spotted Vin's blue Jaguar pulled into a parking bay outside the hotel. They watched Vin lock the car and walk up the steps of the hotel to the imposing entrance. They looked at each other. The same thought had occurred to them and without hesitation, they crossed the road and approached the hotel.

'On arriving outside the hotel, Vin found that he wasn't as confident as he should have been. He remembered Elliot had warned him about Radnitz. Elliot had said: "He's big time and dangerous. He could put you on the ball of his thumb and make a smear of you on a wall." Although Vin had scoffed at this, it had made an impression on him and now that he was about to come face to face with Radnitz he felt uneasy. He would be crazy, he told himself as he drove along Paradise Boulevard, to take the stamps into the hotel. Radnitz might have a gunman around who would take the stamps off him and then throw him out. This would have been Vin's mode of operation had he been in Radnitz's place. He pulled up by the kerb and taking the plastic envelope containing the stamps from his pocket, he lifted the floor mat of the car and slid the envelope out of sight. He refixed the mat, telling himself no one would think to look in that hiding place.' Here, Barney paused to look scornful. 'I'm sure a gentleman of your intelligence, Mr Campbell, would never leave stamps worth a million dollars in your car. You would take in the possibility of the car being stolen, but Vin, as I have already pointed out, had little intelligence and was a slow thinker. So that's what he did.'

'And now,' I said, 'you're going to tell me the car was stolen?'

Barney gave me a glassy stare, hitched himself forward and ignoring my interruption, went on, 'Vin asked for Mr Radnitz and sent up his name. He wasn't kept waiting and this did something for his wilting confidence. Radnitz received him in his big living-room.

'As soon as Holtz had shut the door, leaving the two men alone, Radnitz said abruptly, "You have the stamps?"

' "I have them. You're offering a million dollars for them right?"

'Radnitz nodded.

' "Before parting with them," Vin said, still very unsure of himself, "I want the money credited to my bank in New York."

' "That can be arranged," Radnitz said and held out his hand. "Show me the stamps."

' "You don't imagine I have them with me," Vin said, forcing a grin. "I don't trust anyone. We'll meet at your bank this afternoon. That'll give me time to get the stamps from where I'm keeping them. Before a witness, I'll show you the stamps, you will then instruct your bank to telex my bank in New York, crediting me with a million dollars and then you get the stamps, but not before."

191

'Radnitz regarded him and the chill in his toadlike eyes made Vin shift uneasily.

' "Very well," he said. "Come to the California & Mutual Bank at three o'clock. Ask for Mr Sanderson." He paused, then went on, "Describe these stamps to me."

'Vin described the stamps.

' "There are eight of them?" Radnitz asked.

' "Yeah." Vin found it hard to believe that this man seemed so unconcerned about paying this enormous sum without some quibble. He wondered if he dare try to up the price, but there was something about Radnitz that scared him. After all, he told himself, sweating with excitement, a million, goddamn it! was a million!

' "I must warn you that if you don't produce the stamps and you are wasting my time," Radnitz went on in his quiet guttural voice, "I will make you wish you had never been born."

'This threat shook Vin.

' "You give me the money and I'll give you the stamps."

' "Then at three o'clock this afteinoon," Radnitz said and made a gesture of dismissal.

'Vin took the express elevator to the ground floor. What a mug Elliot was! he thought. All this fuss! This rich punk hadn't hesitated, hadn't even quibbled about paying for the stamps. He was so elated that he wanted to dance a jig. As the elevator doors swished open, he glanced at his watch. The time was 12.56. He had two hours to kill. What did a man do to kill time when he was worth a million dollars? Vin asked himself and he knew the answer: a man bought himself a drink and a fancy meal, and that's what he was going to do. He took out his billfold and checked his money. He had twenty-five dollars: all the money he owned.

He would blow the lot on a slap up meal. Why should he worry? In two hours he would be worth a million!

'Unaware that Larry, half hidden behind an open newspaper, was watching him, Vin strode into the bar and called for a double whisky on the rocks. While waiting, he beckoned to a waiter and told him he wanted a table in the restaurant. The waiter said this could be arranged.

'Larry had moved to the bar entrance and had overheard the conversation. He walked briskly across the lobby and out into the sunshine where Robo was waiting.

' "He's going to stuff his gut," Larry said. "We've lots of time. There's a drug store down the road. Go, buy a roll of gauze bandage and hurry it up."

'Robo grinned and ran off.

'After his drink, Vin swaggered into the restaurant and was conducted to a single table. The rich clients, shovelling food into their faces, looked at him and raised their eyebrows. This brash, shabbily dressed man wasn't in their class, but Vin couldn't care a goddamn. He sat down and surveyed the crowded restaurant with a sneering little grin. He was as good as any of these slobs, he told himself. In two hours' time he would be worth a million dollars! In a month or so he would have his own house and his yacht. This would be the last time he ate alone. Every dollie within a five mile radius would be fighting for his favours once the word got around how rich he was.

'He was a little dashed that the menu was in French, but the suave Maitre d'hôtel was at his elbow to help him. He finally let the Maitre d'hôtel choose the meal of smoked eel and the breast of chicken in lobster sauce.

'While he was eating, Robo came back from the drug store and joined Larry, waiting at the hotel car park.

'Since these two had been in hospital and had been forced to wash themselves, their long hair and their beards, they now looked as respectable as any of the kids on vacation in the City and no one paid any attention to them as they converged on Vin's Jaguar. With Robo shielding his movements Larry removed the cap on the gas tank, quickly unwound some of the bandage and inserted one end into the tank. He then paid out a long length of bandage which he concealed under the car. All this was a work of seconds. Striking a match, he set fire to the gauze which began to smoulder, running up the length of the bandage towards the gas tank.

'They had about two minutes to get clear which was ample time. By the time they had reached some distant clump of palm trees, the Jaguar's gas tank, along with a million dollars' worth of stamps, went up with a bang, shattering some of the hotel's windows.'

*   *   *

'Well now, Mr Campbell,' Barney said, 'that's about the whole story.' He looked at his empty glass and then at the wall clock opposite him. The hands pointed to 02.15. 'It's getting past my bed time.'

'There are still some loose ends to tie up,' I said. 'How about one for the road? I'm having a whisky. How about you?'

Barney's little red snapper of a mouth moved into a smile.

'I've never said no to a drop of Scotch,' he said and flapped with his enormous hand in Sam's direction.

'First, what happened to Judy Larrimore?' I asked.

Barney's fat face showed his disapproval.

'You'll find her at the Adam & Eve club any time you look in there. She's just the same ... looking for boys with money, maybe a little fatter, maybe a little less attractive, but still in the same old groove.'

Sam came over and took the order for whiskies.

'And Vin?'

'I don't have to tell you that Vin flipped his lid when the doorman came into the restaurant asking if anyone owned a blue Jaguar with New York plates. The way Vin rushed out of the restaurant lowered all records for the hundred yards sprint. The sight that met his eyes turned him to stone. The car was a complete write off and he realized his dream of a million dollars was now just a dream. He stood there, white faced, scarcely breathing, watched from a safe distance by Larry and Robo who were squirming with joy. Then a hand on his arm made him turn. Holtz, by his side, asked quietly, "The stamps were in the car?"

'Vin nodded dumbly.

' "Then I am sorry for you," Holtz said and returned to the hotel to report to Radnitz.

'Later, the cops picked Vin up as he was trying to hitch a ride to Jacksonville. Without money, without even his few belongings, he was in trouble. The cops had received a tip off and I don't have to tell you from whom the tip had come. The Miami hotel dick picked Vin out at an identity parade and Vin went away for five years: robbery with violence.'

Sam came with the whiskies. With drunken dignity, Barney leaned forward, tapping his glass against mine.

'Your health, Mr Campbell,' he said. 'Your very good health.'

'And Elliot?' I was wondering if the whisky would prove too much for Barney and I wouldn't hear the end of this story, but I needn't have worried: Barney's capacity seemed without limit.

'Elliot?' Barney lifted his heavy shoulders. 'You didn't read about it? When Joey told him and Cindy what he had done and why, and when Elliot realized there would be no more money coming to him, he gave a wry grin, shrugged and told Joey he had done the right thing.

'Joey wasn't interested in what Elliot thought. He was only concerned to see how Cindy reacted. She sat there, looking at Elliot, and the expression in her eyes made Joey feel bad, but he kept reminding himself that she was young, and in another year, maybe less, she would have forgotten Elliot.

'Elliot said he would now go to Hollywood. There was still a chance that his agent would find work for him. Neither he, Cindy nor Joey believed this, but they went along with it. Elliot shook hands with Joey and wished him luck. He said he hadn't ever enjoyed anyone's company as much as his. This pleased Joey because Elliot said it as if he meant it. Then Elliot turned to Cindy.

' "I told you, Cindy," he said, "we're not for each other. Forget me ..." He smiled at her. "So long."

'He left the bungalow without touching her and Cindy, in her despair, hid her face in her hands and sobbed her heart out.

'Joey didn't attempt to console her. He went to the window and watched Elliot get in the Alfa and drive away. He remembered what Cindy had told him. Elliot had said to her: "You're dead without money." As the Alfa disappeared around the corner, Joey said goodbye to Elliot forever.'

Barney finished his whisky and released a sigh of contentment.

'On the way to Hollywood, Elliot's Alfa was hit by a car driven by a drunk. He was killed instantly.' Barney sniffed and wiped the end of his nose with the back of his wrist. 'The drunk swore to the cops that Elliot had plenty of room to avoid him but who's going to believe a drunk? Anyway, the smash saved Elliot from taking his own life, and if you are to believe what was said about him, that was what he was planning to do.' Barney paused, then shook his head. 'Fate's funny, isn't it?'

'You could say that,' I said. 'And Cindy and Joey … are they still working the City?'

'Oh, no.' Barney shook his head. 'Cindy and Joey are in Carmel. They own a nice little bungalow and they don't steal any more. They are now what you call respectable folk. Joey looks after the bungalow, cuts the lawn twice a week and does the shopping. Cindy has a job at a very decent hotel: a receptionist, I think they call it. From what I hear – and you know by now, Mr Campbell that I'm a guy with his ear to the ground – she's as happy as any pretty girl can be without a husband.'

This didn't quite add up to me.

'How come they own a bungalow in Carmel?' I asked.

Barney suppressed a belch. He looked at his empty glass and sighed.

'Have just one more for the road, Barney,' I said. 'Let's tie up all the loose ends before we call it a night.'

'That's a good idea, Mr Campbell,' Barney said and flip flapped with his hand. Sam brought two more whiskies.

'Almost another story,' Barney said, fondling his glass and wagging his head. 'An hour after Elliot had left, with Cindy crying her eyes out and Joey now trying to console her, a chauffeur driven car pulled up outside the bungalow. An elderly man got out and rang the bell.

'Startled, Joey opened the door.

' "My name is Paul Larrimore," the man said. "There's a young lady living here, I believe … I want to see her."

'Poor Joey felt a chill run up his spine. He had visions of tough cops arriving and taking Cindy and himself to jail.

'Cindy came to the door. Miserably, she tried to smile at Larrimore.

' "I'm sorry," she said. "I took your stamps. I know I shouldn't have done it."

'Joey felt quite sick that Cindy could be so stupid, but Larrimore just smiled and asked if he could come in. So they let him in and Joey saw Larrimore was carrying the old stamp album Cindy had left him.

' "Don't apologize," Larrimore said as soon as he had sat down. "You saved me from a lot of trouble. I would never have had the moral courage to have parted with those stamps and sooner or later they would have got me into trouble. Taking them as you did has saved me from a possible prison sentence. I hope you haven't got them any longer?"

' "No. Mr Larrimore. Someone has sold them," Cindy told him.

' "I don't envy the person who has bought them." Larrimore shrugged. "But never mind, so long as you can't get into trouble." He paused, then he put the old stamp album on the table. "I've brought your album back. Looking more carefully through it, I have found a rare stamp: a misprint. I want it and I will pay you twelve thousand dollars for the stamp and the album." '

Barney finished his drink.

'That's how they bought the bungalow at Carmel, Mr Campbell. Funny how things work out, isn't it?' He yawned and stretched. 'Well, I guess it's my bed time.' Lowering his great arms, he squinted at me. 'Let me remind you, there's not much – if anything – I don't know about this City. When you want to hear another story, you know where to find me.'

I sat for a moment thinking, then I thanked him.

'Sad about Elliot,' I said.

Barney wrinkled his fat nose.

'He's better off dead, Mr Campbell. People who can't manage their money don't get any sympathy from me.' He peered at me. 'You did say another twenty dollars, Mr Campbell? That's what you gave me last time.'

'Did I?' I gave him a twenty dollar bill. 'Well you can't say you don't manage your money, Barney, can you?'

'That's right.' He tucked the bill away in his hip pocket and heaved himself to his feet. 'Good night, mister: pleasant dreams.'

I watched him lumber across the bar and out into the hot, starlit night, then I went over and settled the bill with Sam.

THE END

9 781471 903786